I0619283

INDIANAPOLIS

Praise for
Same Song, Different Beat

"Ronin Heck's grasp of grotesque future lunacy rivals the very best of Philip K. Dick. It is bleak, achingly vivid and deeply provocative. Like all effective dystopian works, its imagined tomorrow reminds us a lot of today."

—David Copper

"A deliciously dark and gripping post-apocalyptic tale reminiscent of Philip K Dick."

—Mark Richardson

"Grinding and hitching through the trash heaps of a near-future America, Heck summons a putrid-scented world of misguided desire, confusion, and societal brain rot. *Same Song, Different Beat* exists in that same special category of creative work that includes Dan Erickson's *Severance*, David Lynch's *Lost Highway*, and Charlie Kaufman's *Antkind.*"

—Colin Jones

SAME SONG,
DIFFERENT BEAT

by
RONIN HECK

"If you don't want a man unhappy politically, don't give him two sides to a question to worry him; give him one."

Ray Bradbury
Fahrenheit 451

The radio on the transport should have been louder. Teo Paz could still hear the ringing. Normally, the high-pitched hum vibrating behind his left ear vanished the moment any form of popular entertainment occupied his thoughts. The DJ introduced the song as Suzanne Minassian's latest version of "Sunshine Manifesto." The DJ claimed the beat had been modified. Suzanne's vocal had not been altered. Teo found it impossible to determine whether any aspect of the song had changed since it usually played at volumes quelling the chance for conversation with his fellow workers on the bus.

He stared out the window, hoped the scenery might distract him from the ringing. The bus turned onto Van Ness and rolled past the district garbage heap, a mountain of trash sitting on the old Hollywood Forever cemetery. Level one workers climbed the peak's spiral foot path with sturdy hemp bags strapped to their backs. They scoured the refuse for anything eligible for the recycling plant. Some had been tasked with removing coveralls from expired workers. They constantly wiped their noses, presumably to combat the stench of rot and decay. It reminded Teo how lucky he'd been to move into level three on account of his veteran status. He'd worked the garbage hill briefly, right after the war. He'd sloshed over moist, empty boxes of food and human and animal remains, day after day. Any time the smell of death compelled him to complain, he'd stare past the trash, at the abandoned buildings in downtown L.A. and the smokestacks and factories just beyond. He'd considered his job superior in that he spent his time on the clock outdoors, breathing what remained of the world's natural air. His positive attitude paid off. Inspectors eventually recommended him for advancement to a higher level.

The transport arrived at Mutual Foods Northwest five minutes before Teo's shift started. He filed off the bus with several colleagues. They waited by the doors for Kang Ji Young, their manager, to let them in. The morning sun bulled through dirty, bloated clouds blanketing South California. Teo tugged at the collar on his coverall. He'd worn his red version. The day before he'd come to work in his blue version. He had a different color for each day of the week. The Mutual Organization referred to this as diversity. The clip on his ID badge dug through the thinning fabric and into his skin. He adjusted it, noted the stark, orange L3 underneath his name, how much nicer it looked than an L1 badge. His hairline in his photograph on the badge reflected how much time had passed since he'd been promoted. The red coverall, apparently, would not hold up much longer. He'd have to buy a new one. Another expense. He tried to hide his disappointment. Like most of the men he knew, he wanted to save his credits for a Cheetah 3000, a sports car Buster Minassian advertised on television every night. The sleek, two-door automobile zipped across ancient highways in other regions. The night before, for instance, Buster had screeched to a halt in front of the ruins of Mount Rushmore. No matter how much Teo tried, however, he couldn't escape nagging bills and personal needs holding his credit balance hostage, stagnant.

And the sun, goodness, did it burn. He preferred not to sweat before stacking boxes on shelves in the market. His face must have revealed his displeasure. Makiko Hana, a young woman who worked in the dessert aisle, approached, her normally pleasant smile strained. She'd worn her purple coverall and painted her eyelids a matching color. "How about this weather?" she said to Teo.

"It's wonderful," he said.

"It is. It is wonderful. Amazing. Amazing and wonderful, yes?" She brushed her shoulder length hair behind her ears. Sweat had formed near her temples. Surely, she didn't enjoy the heat, either.

"Indeed," said Teo. "Wonderful. And amazing." He laughed. "Can we go so far as to say it's wonderfully amazing?"

She played with her hair again. Flirting? She must not have known his situation, how he'd been sterilized after the war, had been barred from procreational privileges. "Did you watch *The Minassians* last night?"

"Yes, yes I did." He didn't have a choice. The ringing in his ear would have driven him insane if not for the television in his apartment. "I like how they got a new actress to play Trudy Minassian."

"Oh, yes!" Makiko's eyes rolled. Her thin lips relaxed. "So, so wonderful. So creative. So amazing."

"Well," said Teo, "you knew one of the daughters would be replaced this week. They spent last week shuffling the parent characters around so much, it only made sense."

"I know, I know," said Makiko. "Trudy has my favorite dialogue, so, you know, it made me really happy to see the producers use her to make the show different."

Teo preferred the previous Trudy. In spite of his sterility, he had desires. He couldn't discuss them. Certainly couldn't act on them. Since the storyline of the television show never changed, he'd lost interest in its dramatic aspects. He fantasized, instead, of making love to one of the many Minassian sisters. Another distraction from the ringing in his ear.

Ji Young unlocked the doors. The staff entered the building in an orderly manner. One by one, they greeted the supervisor:

"Good morning."

"It is a good morning." She'd worn a majestic white, gold-trimmed coverall. The variety of color demonstrated what the writing on her badge confirmed: L5 (though she'd once been a level seven). It also matched the golden earrings she'd worn in the photograph on her badge. She'd wrapped her straight, black hair into a bunch with strands poking out and bobbing anytime she moved her head. "A wonderful, amazing morning, yes?"

"Yes," her employees responded. "A wonderful, wonderful, amazing morning."

When Teo greeted his boss, he could not make eye contact with her. He and Ji Young had an embarrassing history from which he'd never recovered. She'd been decent enough not to discuss it with anyone. Not with the staff and, most importantly, not with any inspectors from the Mutual Organization. Frankly, she should have been grateful *he* hadn't reported *her*. Three years older than him, she had, one day, suggested they engage in unsanctioned procreational activities. She said she'd been rendered infertile by the Mutual Organization. A penalty endured once demoted to a lower level. No one would ever find out. The idea appealed to him. He'd been attracted to his boss since he'd been assigned to her store. But when it came time to engage in the act, he remembered the Mutual physicians assuring him that part of his body no longer functioned for purposes pleasurable or constructive. His body responded, retreated. His boss did her best not to chastise him, make him feel less useful than other men. But she'd also been cold to him forever after. The thrilling tint of unspoken attraction decorating their conversations disappeared.

She greeted him without looking at him and moved on to the next worker in line. Oh well. The last thing anybody wanted? Complaint. He followed his colleague Miguel Pacheco to the stockroom to swipe his ID badge and get to work. Miguel patted him on his shoulder. "You see the new version of the commercial for the Panther 3000 last night?"

"You mean the Cheetah 3000?" he said.

Miguel squeezed the bridge of his nose and closed his eyes. "Pretty sure it's called a Panther, my friend." He shook his head and pinched the ends of a thin mustache he'd recently decided to grow.

Jabbing him with his elbow, Teo said, "No reason to dwell on it. Someday, we will all have the car of our dreams. Just need to keep working." He swiped his ID badge and pulled a shopping cart from a row near the back door. He pushed it around the corner to the stockroom. The front wheels squeaked and wobbled. He read the morning instructions on a clipboard hanging on a hook on the end of the first aisle of vegetable powder. The order called for amber boxes. He loaded his cart with as many as possible and struggled to push it to the vegetable section.

He shoved the remaining flaxen boxes from the day before to the end of the shelf and replaced them with amber boxes. Ji Young turned on the overhead speakers and "Sunshine Manifesto" filled Teo's ears with an electronic, mono-rhythmic beat and a woman's voice singing, "Wonderful, Amazing," over and over again. As Teo continued shelving vegetable powder, the song faded out. A Mutual DJ announced, "Amazing, wonderful! Here's the same song with a different beat." The anthem repeated. Teo couldn't be certain, but it seemed the beats between the two versions of the song had not changed at all. It seemed, in fact, *nothing* had changed. He began to suspect the vocalist had been the same woman singing the song since it had first been produced, just after the war. If he mentioned it, said so out loud, would it be considered a complaint?

As customers filed in, Teo kept the vegetable aisle stocked. A solid wall of amber. The moment a customer grabbed a box, Teo replaced it. He stood on guard, between the stockroom and the vegetable aisle. This represented the amount of authority and responsibility he'd been granted and it constituted the most fulfilling part of his life. On this day, however, he couldn't shake the concern that "Sunshine Manifesto" had been the same song, set to the same beat, since it had become the only legal music in South California. When Ji Young closed the store for a lunch break, Teo decided he had to say something.

In the break room, he sat next to Miguel. As they stirred meat and vegetable powder into a bowl of steaming water, Teo said, in a voice intended for Miguel and no one else, "Have you ever listened to 'Sunshine Manifesto' closely? I mean, really, *really* closely?"

Miguel shrugged. "It's a wonderful song. Amazing." He lifted his spoon to his nose to give the food a whiff.

"And the many different versions," said Teo, "are they really different?"

"My friend…" Miguel put his spoon back in his bowl. "Why would you even ask such a question?"

"A joke," said Teo. "I was joking." He looked around. Makiko Hana had stopped stirring her powder. She stared at him with the concern she'd worn earlier, when she suspected he hadn't enjoyed waiting outside, in the heat. "I wasn't serious," he said. Same explanation, different words. Did she buy it? Would she forget all she'd seen that day?

Following lunch, Ji Young led the staff on a forty-five-minute walk in a circle around the building. The Mutual

Organization referred to this as recess. This allowed the workers to simultaneously digest their food and exercise. Then the market reopened and Teo resumed stocking shelves in the vegetable aisle. More customers showed up as factories and recycling plants let out. People in coveralls much more stained and abused than Teo's or his colleagues' purchased boxes of vegetable and meat powder. Some splurged, apparently not saving for a car or any other luxury item, and bought dessert mixes. Must have been nice. Teo supposed if one had resigned to life in a lower level, why bother attempting to save for something like a Cheetah 3000? Did that qualify as a judgment? He'd have to keep his opinion to himself.

Near closing time, an inspector visited the store. Inspectors walked the aisles, made sure the boxes of food were arranged in an orderly manner. The inspectors would chat with Ji Young. Sometimes they'd strike up conversations with workers. It usually went something like this:

"How's your day been?"

"Amazing. Wonderful. Couldn't ask for more."

"That is amazing. And wonderful. Carry on."

On that day, however, the inspector must have spoken with Makiko. Teo didn't hear the conversation. He'd been focusing on the song playing on the speakers. The monotonous beat drove him up and down the aisle, filling gaps on the shelves with fresh boxes of vegetable powder. The inspector rounded the corner from the dairy aisle and asked to speak with him. No formal greeting, no questions about how things were going. The inspector said, "Teo Paz? Let's step into the break room for a moment." At that point, Teo understood someone had voiced concern. Makiko, he assumed, though his conscience suggested he jump to no conclusions.

The inspector offered him a place at the lunch table. He sat opposite him, allowing Teo to read his ID badge: Claude Ramirez. Had he ever seen this inspector before? So many of them looked alike. They wore gray, lifeless coveralls. Same attitude, different names. Claude Ramirez said, "I understand you've been questioning the authenticity of the latest rendition of 'Sunshine Manifesto.'"

Teo shook his head. "No, no." How honest should he be? He didn't remember much of the war, but he did recall the whole thing being fought over certain people, people he agreed with, insisting their opponents had no integrity. They couldn't be trusted. They told lies. They'd lied about history. They'd lied about contemporary society. They'd lied about the future. He said, "I can't really tell if the beat is different. You know, from one version to the next."

Claude Ramirez relaxed his shoulders. He leaned back in his chair and folded his hands across his chest. "Mr. Paz, have you counted the beats per minute?"

Teo admitted he had not.

"Let me give you an example," said Claude Ramirez. "Do you remember last week's version? The previous Trudy Minassian sang it. That version had one hundred and twenty beats per minute. The new version, Suzanne Minassian's version, has one hundred and twenty-*two* beats per minute. I'd be happy to take you to the studio it was manufactured in and have an engineer demonstrate the difference."

Goodness. Teo admonished himself for having spoken up in the first place. "I'll take your word for it."

This seemed to please Claude Ramirez. He smiled and bobbed his head. "Good, good." He leaned forward once more. He removed his glasses and squinted at Teo's badge. "I see you're a veteran. If the Mutual Organization hasn't thanked you for your service, allow me to do so now."

"Well," said Teo, "thank you, sir."

The inspector smacked the table with an open hand. "I wasn't able to fight in the war. Allergies." He pinched his nose. "We owe this wonderful, amazing society we've built to the sacrifices made by men such as yourself."

"Well," Teo said again, "thank you, thank you. I appreciate that."

In a lower voice, the inspector said, "You owe it to yourself, soldier, to refrain from thinking too much." He tapped his finger against the side of his head. "Let's not forget how thinking led to the war in the first place. Such needless, horrific bloodshed. All because a few powerful people had differing opinions and refused to compromise."

On this, Teo could not have agreed more. He'd been young when the war started, but he'd been old enough to understand things might not go so well for him or others in his generation. The old men bickered. The young men duked it out. But these were negative thoughts, they only led to negative emotions. He promised the inspector he'd stop himself the moment he *suspected* he might start thinking.

"Amazing." Claud Ramirez slapped the table again and stood. "Wonderful. Just remember, we provide all the entertainment you need to occupy that space between your ears." This time, he pointed with two fingers to his eyes and then to Teo's eyes.

Teo took to his feet as well. "Yes," he said. "And it's amazing. Television, the radio. These things are wonderful, amazing."

The inspector rounded the table and patted Teo on his shoulder. "Now you're talking."

As they walked to the front of the store, Teo thought he noticed the inspector's smile vanish, for just a moment, as the inspector wished him well and said goodbye. He returned to the vegetable aisle to stack boxes. All the while, he kept his attention on the inspector. Claude Ramirez had, for some reason, felt the need to confer with Ji Young. They spoke in hushed voices. On several occasions, Ji Young looked over at Teo. She did not project anything he could interpret as positive or encouraging.

When the five o'clock alarm sounded from the charred Hollywood Hills, Ji Young put her hand on Teo's chest. Her bright, red fingernails must have cost her plenty. Most women seemed to spend their extra credits on such frivolous items. For whatever reason, they didn't cultivate desire for something as glorious as the Cheetah 3000. He felt the warmth of her body through her touch. It reminded him of the night they'd attempted recreational procreation. Despite her proximity, he still couldn't look her in the eye. He'd failed her, and the memory led to nothing but miserable thoughts. She said, "You need to watch your comments in public." If anyone understood the danger of revealing too much to other people, it would certainly be her. She told Teo, once, how she'd been a level seven after the war. When he asked her why she'd been demoted, she said she'd offered a superior an opinion she shouldn't have. She wouldn't reveal anything else. "That inspector is *very* suspicious. Whether you like 'Sunshine Manifesto' or not is irrelevant. That's the song we're allowed to play. Imagine stocking shelves without music in the background, how crowded your head would be with thoughts. Useless thoughts." When he opened his mouth to speak, she moved her hand from his chest to his lips. He tasted salt on her fingers. She said, "Thinking is the reason you couldn't please me, remember?"

This cut him like a blade jabbed into his throat and dragged to his belly. This Ji Young, this woman of such brutal honesty, differed so much from the boss Ji Young who roamed the aisles, day after day, offering the same, encouraging words to the workers ("You're doing a wonderful job. Amazing."). How did she separate these two people within her? He still wanted to make love to her and he knew she'd never give him a second chance. And why should she? Why should she risk it? Different night, same humiliation. "Okay," he finally said. "I'll keep my mouth shut."

"There's a good boy." She snagged a quick peek out the doors and then gave him a peck on the cheek. "I don't want you to have to go back to the garbage heap."

"Thank you." Did he blush as she wiped her lipstick from his face?

They walked to the corner to wait for a transport with the rest of the workers. The sun hadn't let up since the morning. Teo Paz stood still, a forced smile on his face, no different from anyone else around him.

Once he returned to his apartment, the ringing in his ear increased. With the rising volume came a hint of pain, like a needle, poking into his jawbone. He turned on the television hanging on the far wall of the living room. The Mutual News broadcast had already started. Pictures of smoggy, hazy, filthy, disgusting North California filled the screen. Wilma Minassian's voice narrated the usual story about misery beyond the border. "The tribes of Old San Fran," she said, "set fire to the Wharf district yet again." She said the unrest had resulted from lack of a central, organizing structure in the region.

Teo opened new boxes of powdered vegetables and powdered meat, mixed them in a bowl, and ran steaming water from the faucet in his tiny kitchen over the grains until they thickened into a brown sludge. He stirred it with a spoon and then sat down to watch the rest of the news. Same stories, different day.

As he finished his dinner, a sports program replaced the news. It must have been Wednesday. The game involved two teams attempting to throw a ball into a hole on their opponent's side of a gymnasium. The balls and the goals this week were smaller than the previous week's. Same game, different balls.

A crowd watching the competition cheered no matter which side scored. Teo could never keep track of who nabbed the most goals. At the end of each contest, both teams were declared winners by default. This kept everyone, the players and the audience, happy. No matter how loud the cheering got, however, Teo could not stop focusing on the ringing in his ear. He turned the volume on his television as high as it would go. He put his head next to one of the speakers on the bottom of the TV during a commercial for the Cheetah 3000. The engine roared, but it did not stop the siren wailing in the back of his mind. He focused on the actual Cheetah, a sleek cat capable of escaping anything, running, super-imposed, in the background of the commercial.

The latest version of the Minassian's situation comedy started after the sports program. Again, Teo jammed his ear against the speaker in hopes the laugh track would drown out the ringing. A headache developed. He could no longer sit on his plush, three-cushioned couch and watch television. He stormed out his door and through the hallway to a steel fire escape he often used as a balcony to enjoy the cool, South California night air. He caught himself on the railing and tried to slow his breathing. His vision doubled from the pounding down the center of his skull. On the sidewalk below, he thought he saw an inspector, just standing there, hands in the large pockets on the sides of his gray coverall, staring up at him, as though he knew him. Teo grabbed his forehead with his hands and squeezed. This gesture, he believed, would simmer the throbbing in his brain. It would align his vision. When he looked at the sidewalk once more, the man in the gray coverall had disappeared.

Teo struggled to keep a positive attitude the next morning. He'd barely slept. Most of the evening, he jammed a finger or a thumb into his ear, thinking it would quell the ringing. As the night progressed, the ringing expanded, grew into a bandwidth wrapping around his skull. He flipped from his left side to his right, cramming his head into his pillow. Had his neighbors or colleagues, or worse, an inspector, witnessed his antisocial behavior, he would have been recommended for psychiatric evaluation. He'd endured one after the war. The result? Sterilization. What a ghoulish process—sitting on the other side of a desk answering senseless questions while a former college professor made wild judgments and accusations. Teo had been deemed too aggressive for breeding purposes. And who'd made him so? Who'd put a weapon in his hand and told him to squeeze the trigger? The same woman who'd evaluated him.

No, no. Mustn't think. His face would betray his anger. He focused on the song playing on the transport's speakers. "*Wonderful...Amazing...*" Which Minassian sang it? He couldn't differentiate Suzanne, Trudy, or Kitty's voice.

A man in a gray coverall near the front of the bus stared at him. Teo didn't like this sort of behavior, strangers just gawking at him. He looked over his shoulder, then at the man—*You couldn't possibly be interested in me*. This did nothing to thwart the man's gaze. Pale features. Glasses. Similar to the glasses Claude Ramirez wore. Teo focused on the garbage mountain as the bus passed it. His anger at the gawker diminished the ringing in his ears. If he thanked the stranger, would that demonstrate good will on his part?

Stop thinking.

The bus arrived at the market. He wove through the exiting crowd. He slowed as he approached the doors. Miguel and Makiko stood together. They nodded. He wanted to wince from the pain in his skull, but refrained. He'd caused enough suspicion. He marched with his colleagues into the store, his smile feeling like a mask. To his boss, he said, "Wonderful, wonderful, wonderful, amazing morning."

Ji Young said, "Well, this is amazing. And wonderful."

He swiped his ID badge, made sure he collected as many credits as possible for his time. The ringing in his ear became a butcher's knife, jabbed into the hinge holding his jaw to the rest of his skull. He wanted to scream. He grabbed a cart, one with smoother wheels than the cart he'd used the previous day. The order sheet in the stockroom called for daffodil vegetable boxes. As he went to work replacing the amber boxes on the shelves with the new ones, he begged, in his mind, for Ji Young to hurry and turn on the radio. When she did, the DJ announced, "Brand spanking new version of 'Sunshine Manifesto.' Here's the matriarch of the family, Gertrude Minassian, giving us the same song, with different vocals." The elder woman crooned over scratchy dents in her voice caused by cigarettes she'd smoked before the war. Teo could not deny this version of the song veered from the usual. But the music, even at the unnerving volume Ji Young set it to, failed to distract him from the ringing in his ear. The headache he'd nursed since the night before blossomed into a sensation he could only compare to what a dead body must feel like as rot and decay chiseled away at it. He remembered, briefly, being a child, just before the war, playing with a model train set with his father. His father brought home Styrofoam, an outlawed substance in South California, and showed him how to break it into pieces, glue it to the plywood board he'd nailed the train tracks to, and assault it with brown spray paint. The paint crumpled and dissolved the edges of the Styrofoam until they resembled mountains and hillsides. He imagined his brain looked the same, right then. As he raised a box of vegetable powder to place it on the shelf, he lost control of his motor skills and dropped it. His knees buckled and he smacked his head on a shelf as he collapsed. The ringing in his ear became a chase, a manic wail running round and round in his skull. His vision ping-ponged and he tilted to the side as he tried to get to his feet. He had to hold on to the shelf as he made his way, carefully, to the front counter, where Ji Young worked the machine deducting credits from customers purchasing food powder. Before his palms landed on the counter, she said, "Teo, are you having trouble?"

He grabbed his forehead, squeezed. "I think I need to visit health services."

Ji Young put her hand on his shoulder. "You'll lose credits for not working."

"I don't have a choice."

The closest Mutual Health facility occupied an eleven-story building near MacArthur Park, on the corner of Wilshire and South Alvarado. Teo walked there from Third Street. Several level one workers hustled back and forth, using electric rods to zap black rats the size of dogs. They placed the rodents' convulsing bodies in cloth sacks hung over their shoulders. One worker decided to play with a rat, kicking it down the sidewalk like a sports ball. The animal squealed. Its panicked protest mimicked the ringing in Teo's ear. As the worker cornered the rat at a concrete bench, the rat jumped onto the bench. It hopped up on a wall and through iron posts in a fence surrounding a condemned apartment complex. The level one must have seen the look of disgust on Teo's face. He said, "I guess that seemed negative."

"Where's the health facility?" Teo said.

The level one pointed to a white building with blue-trimmed windows. "If you enter through the side door, the delivery entrance," said the level one, "you might be able to sneak into the line a little closer to the first desk."

"Thank you," said Teo. The guy would never surpass level one. No integrity, no sense of ethics. But, no need to judge him. Developing negative opinions of others' behavior added nothing positive to his own life. At least, that's what the Mutual Organization preached during commercial breaks on television and the radio.

He walked down the sloped street. The concrete hadn't been maintained since the war. Yellow grass peeked through cracks in the pavement. The road never endured stress beyond a transport bus rolling over it once or twice an hour or the occasional inspector driving a beige Mutual van. As he turned the corner, he saw the line of people waiting to consult with a health professional. Hopefully, the level fives at the desks inside knew what they were doing, knew how to move things along. He took his place behind a woman in a lavender coverall. Short, blonde hair and turquois eyes. She reminded him of postcards he'd seen of tropical islands. She gave him a polite smile and stepped forward. "Wonderful day," she said.

"Wonderful," he said. "Amazing."

"Yes," she said. "Amazing." She turned around and faced the man in front of her.

Weeds blanketed MacArthur Park. Dead trees. Craters filled with yellow grass indicated where ponds, or lakes, as they'd been called by more optimistic people, had once been. Vines covered the signs at the edges of the sidewalks, signs designating the area historic. For whatever reason, the Mutual Organization felt no need to maintain the park. Too bad. It could have provided the kind of entertainment that could never be called the same. Teo remembered visiting similar places with his father. They'd fed bread to ducks swimming on the lake and waddling onto shore. He couldn't imagine what a child growing up in the world after the war felt like. Did young people even know the *word* imagination?

You're thinking too much.

Two, then three people entered the facility. Good. He'd probably go with the next group. The afternoon sun bore down like a heavy quilt. It reflected off solar panels atop the roofs of every building. A silver sheen splashed across the gray sky. When no one appeared to be watching him, he wiped sweat from his forehead. Between the ringing in his ear and the unbearable heat, his brain boiled. He imagined it *breathing*, like a lung. A level five at the door let him and two others into the facility. The level five wore a pink coverall, something rare, and spoke in a voice almost as pleasant as the women who sang "Sunshine Manifesto." She looked at his badge and said, "What's your trouble?"

He described the ringing in his ear, the pounding between his temples.

"Sounds physical, not psychological." The level five handed him a ticket with a crimson number twenty-three on it. "Follow the red line." She pointed to a strip of tape on the dirt-caked tiles. "Preliminary screening. Third floor."

The red line led to a massive room filled with industrial office desks and level five interviewers behind them. Those seeking audience with an interviewer occupied twelve rows of folding chairs. Teo sat down. An artificial source cooled the air. Nicer than his apartment. A neon display hanging above the rows of chairs flashed a number nine. A voice barked over a sound system, briefly interrupting an orchestral version of "Sunshine Manifesto." Same song, different instrumentation. The voice said, "Now serving number nine. Number nine, now serving."

A man in the second row stood and approached the first desk. The woman behind the desk directed him to another counselor, deeper in the pool of desks. Teo forced himself to smile. How many credits would he lose, just sitting there? It seemed the Mutual Organization had not thoroughly thought out this system. He remembered the nightly news broadcasts, however, reminding him how savage things had gotten in the north. A little chaos had to be better than complete anarchy. He put his fingers to his temples and rubbed the sides of his skull. If anyone asked, he'd talk about his headache. That surely couldn't be perceived as a complaint. Most of the people around him seemed preoccupied with their own troubles. A woman several seats to his left patted her belly. A stomach issue or, perhaps, pregnant. He tried to peek at her ID badge. Procreational activities required a level seven or higher. The woman caught him staring. She said, "Wonderful day, yes?"

"Oh, yes," said Teo. "Wonderful. Amazing."

"Yes," she said. "Amazing."

He decided to mind his own business. Old fashioned behavior, for sure. After what seemed an hour, his number flashed on the neon display. The announcer called it out on the speakers. Teo asked the level five at the first desk where he should go. She pointed. "Talk with Cathy," she said.

Teo sat down at the desk indicated. He read the level seven's ID badge: Cathy Moon. Her black coverall clung to her form and made Teo, once again, sad he'd been barred from procreational privileges. Her long, dark hair settled over her shoulders and framed her young, square face. She smiled and said, "Wonderful day, yes?"

"Wonderful." Teo folded his hands to keep from looking nervous.

"And what's your trouble?" She flipped a piece of paper over a clipboard and held a pen ready to write.

"Well, I've had a ringing in my ear since the war." He tilted his head to the left, indicating which ear had been afflicted.

Cathy Moon leaned forward. She must have spent most of her extra credits on beauty products. A wave of citrus perfume travelled across the desk. "Mr. Paz, yes?"

He nodded.

"Mr. Paz," she said, "we thank you so much for your service."

People said this to him all the time. It rarely sounded meaningful. "My pleasure." The war had most certainly *not* been a pleasure. "Anyway," he said, "I can usually drown out the ringing with music or the television. Yesterday, or, to be precise, last night, the ringing increased. It's become intolerable, to be honest."

"Oh, my…" Cathy Moon drew in her face. "We cannot tolerate intolerance."

"Exactly."

"Unfortunately," she said, "a ringing in the ear doesn't represent a situation of urgent need. We could probably schedule you for an appointment with a doctor in…" She flipped through a ledger to her right. "Looks like I can get you in with Dr. Izaki in twenty-one days." Her clamped jaw suggested debate also intolerable.

"Ah…" Teo grabbed his forehead. "Yeah, you see, it's causing a massive headache. Like, I can't function. I can't work. Twenty-one days…no. That's too, that's amazingly way out there."

21

She relaxed. "Well, now we're talking something else. Work-inhibiting pain *does* qualify for an emergency diagnosis." She studied her ledger again. This time, she perused several pages in the back. "I can send you straight up to the eleventh floor. That will cost you forty-five credits, just so you know."

Where did it end? Did they want him to work, or not? How long would it take to recover from this hit before he could start saving, once more, for a Cheetah 3000? A thunderbolt of pain rocked his skull from left to right. He said, "Wonderful."

She passed him the clipboard and pointed to a line underneath a slew of notes she'd scribbled in handwriting he couldn't decipher. "Autograph here."

He did so.

"Wonderful," she said. "Amazing. Now…" She directed his attention to the hallway. "Take the green staircase to the eleventh floor." She motioned for him to give her his badge. "Thank you." She swiped the badge on a small machine resembling a calculator from the old world.

Teo followed several people up the green steps. By the time he arrived at the top floor, his breathing staggered, clawed for air. Pleasant chemicals flowed from his brain and alleviated, for a moment, both the ringing in his ear and the headache. He worried he might not have evidence to provide the doctor. This proved a needless concern after he'd been given another number and told to sit amongst another batch of folding chairs. The eleventh floor differed, however, in that past the receptionist's desk, workers were directed to specific doors lining a narrow corridor. Teo sniffed the air. The stench of chemicals employed to sterilize medical instruments. Reminded him of soap he'd used to wash his hands and arms after a day on the garbage heap, when he'd still been a level one. The pain returned, a band saw slicing off the top of his skull.

The sun travelled from windows on one side of the waiting room to the other. It must have been close to quitting time at the market. He'd lost an entire day. Before the war, he'd entertained an extensive vocabulary suitable for negative situations, for expressing displeasure. These words often eased the suffering caused by life's constant trials. The Mutual Organization legislated consequences for using such language. The most obvious, of course, being a level reduction affecting one's credits and overall lifestyle. It didn't take long to whittle communication to two words:

Wonderful.

Amazing.

And nothing else.

How good it would feel to open the chest of forbidden terms and shout, right there in the waiting room. Something like, "Goddammit!" That would have incurred two penalties, one for the profanity and one for the allusion to religion, outlawed following the war. But Teo only sighed. Quiet as possible. He placed his hands on his knees and stared straight ahead. "Sunshine Manifesto" filled his ears, encouraged him to stay positive. He carried a thin, patient smile to the receptionist's desk upon hearing his number. The man behind the desk instructed him to take his troubles to room nineteen. He said, "It's a pleasant hike down the hallway." He pointed, as though Teo could not figure out where to go next. "Have a wonderful visit with the doctor."

"I will," said Teo. "I'm sure it will be amazing."

"Yes," said the receptionist. "Amazing."

The corridor ran long and, the further Teo walked down it, the darker it got. Small lights, the kind his parents used to drape over a tree when they still celebrated Christmas, decorated every other door. He found nineteen, knocked, and entered.

Health professionals wore white coveralls. The woman waiting for him in room nineteen had gray, curly hair. She'd somehow survived the civil war. Most of the elders committed assisted suicide. Her aged, wrinkled face, her serene, emerald eyes calmed Teo. She offered her hand. As he shook it, he marveled at the loose, fragile skin over thin, brittle bones. Her badge identified her as Leticia Ortega, a level nine. She gestured for him to sit on a hard, plastic observation table near her desk. "What seems to be your trouble, Mr. Paz?"

He explained. She asked why he hadn't seen anyone sooner to examine his ear. "I don't know," he said. "In the war, I was taught to accept suffering as a part of life. After the war, I was taught to say only positive things, to not complain."

"Well," said the doctor, "that's just silly." She used an instrument to poke inside his left ear. "I don't see anything unusual." She placed her soft hands on his cheeks and applied pressure. She did the same to the sides of his head. Just in front of his left ear, she dug in her thumb, near his temple. "Fascinating." She told him to open his mouth. "I'm going to poke around your jaw, if you don't mind." Without waiting for him to respond, she produced a pair of rubber gloves from a box inside a drawer on her desk. She forced her thumb to the back of his mouth and made a series of noises he assumed denoted curiosity. As she dropped the gloves down a disposal tube, she said, "There's something in your jaw." She sat at her desk and scribbled on a piece of paper attached to a clipboard. "I don't want to cause alarm, but something has calcified near the external acoustic meatus." She must have gleamed Teo's confusion. "Something is there that should not be." She handed him the clipboard. "I'm putting in an order for an x-ray. The fee is hefty, but I think it's necessary."

Oh, for...

No, no. He found the key to that treasure chest of profanity and secured the lock on it. "How much?" he said.

"A full cranium view..." She put a finger to her chin and glanced at the ceiling. "I imagine it'll run you at least eighty to a hundred credits."

This day would cost him nearly a week of work. The exact surplus he'd have after paying usual expenses for the month. Once again, he'd add nothing to his savings for the Cheetah 3000. "You don't think this is temporary?"

"I think you've already answered that question for yourself." The doctor stared at him over the top of her thin-rimmed glasses. "If I were you, I'd have this test done immediately. We don't have many instances of cancer anymore, thanks to the war. But it does show up, every now and then."

Cancer? He hadn't even heard the word since before the war. "Cancer?" he said out loud. The need to be positive vanished. He didn't know much about disease, but he understood cancer represented the worst of the lot. And just how had he gotten it? The powdered food the Mutual Organization had approved had been tested multiple times. Pollution had been contained. He hadn't engaged in procreational activities since before the war. What...the...*hell?*

"What do you say, Mr. Paz?" The doctor nodded at the clipboard. "Head on down to six. They should have time to get you in before closing."

He sighed. "Wonderful," he said. "Amazing." He signed the order and allowed the doctor to tear off a ticket to grant him entrance to the sixth floor.

"Very good." The doctor showed him to the door. "Keep going down this hallway. There's a flight of gold steps that will take you directly to the sixth floor."

The sun set as he waited to be called back for the x-ray. When the receptionist, a level five in a lime coverall, announced his number over the loudspeaker, she swiped his badge to remove the necessary credits and directed him to an office in a well-lit corridor. As he walked, the fluorescents overhead flickered. The power gathered by the panels on the roof during the day must have been waning. He hoped the x-ray machine wouldn't give out before the technician could get an image of his skull. If it did fail, he would require a return trip. More lost hours of work. It would also delay any possible cure the doctors would recommend.

The attendant in the office he'd been sent to looked as though he'd only recently entered the workforce. Teo envied the young man's early success. Did he already own a Cheetah 3000? The level five, identified as Victor Suez, appeared to be growing a full beard, no doubt to hide his youth. He said, "Wonderful evening, yes?"

"Yes," said Teo. "Amazing."

Victor nodded. Dark circles under his eyes suggested he'd been working the entire day. "Yes, amazing. Wonderful." He instructed him to drape a heavy, lead apron hanging on the wall around his chest. "Have a seat." He pointed to a swivel chair situated between several large, beige and black screens. Once Teo had done as asked, Victor exited the room. The black screens circled Teo's head. Tiny pops, like fireworks heard from a distance, exploded eight times during the process. The cameras retreated and Victor returned. "You're free to go back to the eleventh floor. Dr. Ortega will have your x-rays."

Fatigue made the hike up the steps arduous, even annoying. Teo should have been at home, watching television. What if a coworker asked him about the programming tomorrow? He wouldn't be able to respond. Not honestly. The entire day, in fact, had put him in danger of being *different* from his colleagues. Multiple transgressions like that could not only hinder his ability to move to a higher level, it might even result in a reduction to level one.

The wait to see Dr. Ortega didn't last long. The facility had emptied. Only staff and a handful of patients remained. When he entered Dr. Ortega's office, she studied a printout of an x-ray. His, he assumed. She'd removed her thin-rimmed glasses and rubbed the bridge of her nose, as though she were solving a grand puzzle. She had him sit on the table once more. "Mr. Paz," she said, "I'm not really sure what to tell you." She laid out four images of his skull. She pointed to the right side of his head. "Everything looks fine, here." Then she showed him the left side. She tapped her finger on a white oval just behind his ear. "This is artificial. It looks like it's attached to the base of your skull." She scratched her elbow. "How long have you had your trouble, I mean, overall?"

Teo closed his eyes. He tried to remember a time he had *not* heard the ringing in the back of his mind. Had it been there in his youth? No. During the war? He barely remembered the war. "I guess," he said, "it started after the war."

The doctor smacked her lips together. "I see." She gathered the printouts and handed them to him. "I've conferred with the surgeon here in this region and he says there's no way to operate. The device, whatever it is, is situated such that you might not emerge from surgery the same person."

What in the world did that mean?

She must have read his mind. "There could be damage to your brain. Your identity would be unnaturally altered." She

27

nodded at the printouts. "So, officially…" She forced him to make eye contact with her. "Officially," she said, this time with more force, "we can't operate on you. *Officially*, understand?"

"What am I supposed to do about the ringing? The headache?"

She asked for his badge. "I can authorize a painkiller for you. That's about it."

He took a late transport to his apartment. He sat in the back of the bus and stared at the x-ray of the left side of his skull. Had he been shot in the war? Shrapnel? What kind of shabby healthcare had the Mutual Organization designed? What were the credits he paid into the Mutual Health system good for? The ability to contain his desire to complain threatened to disappear.

Teo got home in time to watch the late show, hosted by Hubert Minassian. The actor currently playing Hubert had thick, gray sideburns. He exuded the amiable demeanor previous Huberts had. Same attitude, different actor. Two of his daughters, Trudy and Melissa, and his youngest son Marvin appeared as guests. He sat behind an elegant, mahogany desk with a microphone on it. The old Los Angeles skyline, the skyline from before the war, had been painted on the backdrop. The guests occupied leather seats to the side of Hubert's desk. They discussed what they always discussed: their wonderful, amazing lives. Level thirteens, the Minassians enjoyed luxuries no lower level worker would ever attain. At least, Teo *suspected* this. Were he honest with his neighbors and colleagues, he would have pointed out the Minassians didn't do work of any kind. But he kept his mouth shut.

The day of running up and down the stairs at the health facility had exhausted him. He fell asleep on the couch without pulling out the bed. In the morning, he woke up with the x-ray pictures laying on his chest. The ringing had, somehow, managed to increase. He put his finger in his left ear and scrubbed, wishing the sound a mere stain removed with pressure. The headache became a marathon, a glob of pain circling his brain, just above his eyes. Round and round and round. He'd have to move fast in order to stop in at the

Mutual Drugs Northwest down the road from the market. He prepared breakfast powder, consumed it in a hurry, and showered.

As he walked to the bus stop at Eighth and Lorraine, he noticed people across the street in gray coveralls, standing still, and, as far as he could tell, watching him. Initially, he dismissed them. He glanced at a woman in gray twice. She certainly *seemed* to be glaring at him. Why would a stranger take so much interest? Crossing Norton, he caught sight of a heavy man in a gray coverall sipping from a black coffee cup. The man leaned against a bullet-ridden YIELD sign. Even when he brought the cup to his mouth to drink, his gaze didn't alter. Teo entertained the idea it might be an old comrade from the civil war. Because his memory of the war barely existed, it could be men he'd fought with recognized him even though he did not recognize them. He maintained eye contact with the man, gave him the opportunity to explain his interest in him. But the man did nothing but continue sipping and staring. Sipping and staring. Sipping and staring. Closer to the bus stop, another inspector, a man in gray, sat on the bench, presumably waiting for the transport headed in the opposite direction. He crossed his legs and trained his eyes on Teo. No matter how often Teo looked over his shoulder to suggest the man avert his eyes, the man never glanced in any other direction.

On the bus, Teo considered the people glaring at him tricks of his mind. How could so many strangers take an interest in him? They looked like inspectors. Aside from his suggestion that the Wednesday version of "Sunshine Manifesto" sounded the same as the previous day's version, he hadn't said anything that could be construed as a complaint. Frankly, with all he'd been through, he felt he should be rewarded for his patience. He couldn't imagine most people putting up with the pain he had and not grumbling once or twice. New doubts emerged, however, as he noticed a tall woman in a gray coverall holding on to the safety bar bolted to the roof of the bus, looking at him in a manner suggesting he owed her something. She should have spent credits on medicine for her badly chapped lips. Teo decided he'd call this woman's bluff. He engaged her in a staring contest. His eyes teared and blurred and he had to blink and shake off the vertigo caused by keeping them open for so long. The expression on the woman's face didn't change. He visualized standing, approaching her, and demanding, "What are you looking at?" The consequences would have been disastrous. Wonderfully, amazingly disastrous. He'd be on the garbage heap within twenty-four hours. But something inside begged him to stop playing this game, stop pretending nothing unusual were taking place.

He stood. He put his hand on the safety rail to keep from falling over as the bus dipped and dived between and around bomb craters in the street. He maintained eye contact with the woman as he stepped, little by little, down the aisle. As he got closer to her, she reached over and yanked the cable signaling the driver to make the next stop. The bus pulled to the curb and the front door opened and the woman marched down the steps and onto the sidewalk. She never ceased staring at Teo. He arrived at the front of the bus just as the doors hissed shut and the driver veered the vehicle back onto the road. As the transport passed the woman, the woman continued gawking at Teo.

Had she read his ID badge? Would she report him? He hadn't said anything. He'd only approached her, as though he wanted to confront her. Would that be enough evidence to demote him? He sat down on a bench reserved for old people and pregnant women, two populations rarely seen in South California. The bus driver gave him a sour glance in the rearview mirror. He didn't stick with it, though. Must not

31

have been in on whatever conspiracy the inspectors had hatched against him.

Conspiracy.

No, no. This term had been outlawed before the war. He shook his head, as though that would jettison the word from his mind for good. Maybe the inspectors just wanted to observe him, make sure he stopped questioning the entertainment provided by the Mutual Organization. Without entertainment, what would the workers discuss? They might start generating thoughts and, gosh darn it, he knew what thinking could cause. No way would he contribute to the instigation of another war.

Teo purchased the drugs Dr. Ortega prescribed and popped one into his mouth as he walked to the market. Makiko asked him where he'd been, why he hadn't gone straight to the lot outside the market after getting off the bus. The urge to tell her to mind her own business bubbled in his heart like a desire to scratch a healing wound. He smiled and said, "Health trouble."

"Oh, no," she said. "That's not wonderful at all. What's the trouble?"

Would her vocabulary change if he grabbed her by her shoulders and shook her brain loose? "Severe headache," he said. Until he spoke with Ji Young, the only person he could trust, he didn't feel safe discussing the object attached to his skull. He tried to scoot around Makiko, position himself to be among the first through the doors when they opened.

Moving with him, Makiko said, "Did the doctor suggest breaking habit and walking down the block before coming to work would help your headache?"

Okay. She wanted to dig and dig and dig. How about this: "Actually, she said the main culprit was people asking me too many questions." There. The woman would get the point. She'd have to get it. She couldn't possibly find it appropriate to badger him anymore.

Makiko backed up. Her breathing increased. Her chest heaved. "I think you're being negative." She looked as though she might cry.

Would this never end? Teo turned on the phony politeness once more. "Not at all, Makiko," he said. "Sound is causing this pain, any sound. I'm trying to keep the amount of sound I have to deal with to a minimum. If it makes you feel better, know that right now, the sound of my own voice is killing me."

She shook her head and glided to a group of workers in the middle of the lot. She might be a problem. What would someone have done before the war? Murdered her. Silenced her. He'd killed in the war. Not a satisfying feeling. At least, not from what he could remember.

The doors opened and he followed his coworkers into the building. Ji Young stood at the front counter, offering the usual wonderfuls and amazings. Same greeting, different day. Teo kept his hands in his pockets. He'd folded up the x-rays and stuffed them into the right one. As soon as he could speak with her alone, he'd ask her what she thought he should do. He'd woken up throughout the night, the pain so severe he considered jamming a sharp object into his ear and prying out the object on his own. He couldn't live like this. Eventually, the ringing and the pain would drive him insane.

The drug kicked in just after he started placing honey-colored boxes of vegetable powder on the shelves. It trickled from the back of the skull, down his spine, and throughout his body. The cardboard boxes in his hands felt sensual. The boxes on the shelves, the lights overhead, no longer dull, now vibrant, *alive*. The stale smell of cardboard that had put his nose to sleep since he'd started working in the market now made him think of food. Not the powdered food the

Mutual Organization had approved of, no, he thought of steaks and chicken and pork he'd eaten growing up, before the war. He'd hated vegetables back then, but even a nice bowl of steamed carrots and broccoli would have been wonderful and amazing. And "Sunshine Manifesto," sprinkling from the speakers in the ceiling like a warm rain in what they used to call summertime, oh, nothing could beat it. He *enjoyed* his work. He took his time placing each box on the shelf. Symmetry, suddenly, the meaning of life. Wonderful, amazing symmetry. It took him longer than necessary to empty his cart.

Ji Young must have been watching him. She approached him and whispered, "What's your trouble now?" She scrutinized him. He thought of Dr. Ortega, how free she'd been with her concern.

Best to be honest with the boss. He said to her, "The doctor prescribed some medicine for the headaches. I think it's slowing me down. I apologize."

She spoke a little louder, though, not loud enough workers in the other aisles could hear. "What about the ringing?"

"Oh…" Teo pulled the x-rays from his pocket and showed them to her. "You see this?" He pointed to the bright blotch behind his ear. "Doctor says it's some kind of thing, attached to my skull. Says they can't remove it. Not officially." He held up one finger and emphasized the word officially, the way the doctor had.

Ji Young licked her lips. She leaned in close and said, "You need to get rid of this." She glanced over her shoulders, as though she expected an inspector to drop out of thin air and harass them. "I know someone who can do it. It will be expensive, but it's necessary."

Teo shook his head. "I don't mean to sound negative, but I've already lost too many credits from yesterday's visit to the health facility. The pill I took, it stopped the headache and ringing, I can barely hear it now. I'll just go with the doctor's orders at this point."

His boss walked away, letting her fingers trail across his back. She said, "If you change your mind, let me know."

On the ride home, Teo kept an eye out for nosy strangers on the transport. The passengers seemed preoccupied with the song playing on the speakers. Most of them nodded along to "Sunshine Manifesto." Some muttered the lyrics to themselves:

"Wonderful...Amazing...."

He maintained the same alertness on his walk from the bus stop to his apartment. Could hallucination explain his worries in the morning? He wished he knew and understood more about psychiatry. Then again, he considered, it's possible the pills, of which he had taken three by the end of the workday, clouded his judgment. Possibly even providing a counter-hallucination, blocking out anybody who might look suspicious.

Hadn't Claude Ramirez told him to avoid this? *Thinking.* Teo reminded himself all the conflicts thinking had caused previous generations—the simple-minded ideologies waging war after the 2036 elections. Two tribes determined to impose their points of view on the rest of the country. He hurried to his apartment. The ringing no longer seemed a pressing issue. The danger of following bleak corridors in his mind, however, presented a threat only the television could thwart. He climbed the steps and fumbled his ID badge through the scanner on his door. When he entered his room, he took a deep breath. The very sight of his TV, issued by the Mutual Organization, hanging on his wall, waiting for him like a domestic partner, brought his heart rate to a gentle, sluggish pace.

As he made his way to his kitchen to prepare dinner, he pressed the ON button on the television and opened a cabinet to retrieve near-barren pumpkin-colored boxes of vegetable and meat powder. He emptied them into a bowl and held the bowl under the faucet. Stirring the powder into a crunchy sludge, he noticed the television had not turned on. He returned to the living room. No picture. No sound. He pressed the ON button once more. This time a little harder, as though the machine needed encouragement. He tried to remove the TV, to look at the back of it, as though he would somehow, innately, understand how to repair it. It had been firmly mounted to the wall. Wouldn't budge. He fiddled with the ON button some more, imagining it had a mind of its own and had decided to be stubborn. The screen remained lifeless. A new kind of dread arrived as he considered an evening without entertainment.

The ringing in his ear exploded into an unbearable buzz. He reached into the pocket of his coverall and pulled out the bottle of pills. He dropped two in his hand and swallowed them. Walking to the kitchen to retrieve his dinner felt like battling a blizzard in one of the northern states, where winter sometimes, according to news broadcasts, returned to punish the uncivilized. The noise in his ear throbbed in synch with the pain beating at the inside of his skull, like a wavelength.

Someone must be doing this. Someone must be able to control this thing in my head.

He grabbed his bowl from the kitchen counter and fought his way to the couch to sit down and eat. He forced himself to chew and swallow the sludge.

This food is awful. It's not even food. Why are we pretending otherwise?

No.

No.

No.

He reached for the couch cushions to smash them against the sides of his head, hoping that would quell the storm until the medicine did its job. As his hands wrapped around the edges of the cushions, he stopped. He looked at the couch closer and realized the cushions had been turned upside down. Had he done this? Had he decided, for no apparent reason, to flip the couch cushions before going to work that morning? How could the television have failed right then? He needed to hear the comforting concern of the Mutual News. He needed a Mutual sports program to distract him. He needed to see and hear the vapid Minassian clan discussing where they'd travel to on their yacht next weekend. These things were more important than the pills. They'd filled his brain with so much insolation, without them, he worried a flood of thoughts, many negative, would invade, would make life even more difficult.

He set the bowl of sludge down and left his apartment. He hit the street, rushing past the many lights designed to keep the neighborhood safe and secure. If an inspector caught him, he'd be taken in for a psychiatric evaluation. If a neighbor saw him, the neighbor might alert the Mutual Organization. The same result—he'd be tested, grilled, asked why he didn't behave *exactly* like everyone else.

He held his head to contain the throbbing. He twisted and turned through the streets of Hancock Park and Koreatown, trying to remember where his boss lived. They'd met near the ruins of the Wiltern Theater the night they'd attempted to procreate.

Sex. It's called sex. Why use such a stuffy word for a natural act?

She'd led him somewhere north of Third Street. The new buildings, living quarters constructed after the war, all looked so similar. Pale walls with blackened windows and cast-iron fire escapes trailing down the fronts and backs. He remembered seeing the broken, decayed letters of the Hollywood sign in the hills from Ji Young's apartment.

The drugs kicked in. Landed on his shoulders with the weight of a transport bus. His pace slowed. His vision blurred. As the medicine subdued the thunder and lightning in his head, he closed his eyes and visualized the night he spent with Ji Young. She took him by the hand, led him right, then left, then right to…Of course. She lived on Mariposa.

432 Mariposa.

He forced himself to move faster.

A box in front of her building contained buzzers for the apartments. He found her picture, the same used on her ID badge, and pressed the bell for her door. "Yes?" The tone of her voice suggested she'd been interrupted.

"It's me," said Teo.

She took her time answering. "Don't let anyone see you."

The glass doors beyond the buzzer rattled. Teo opened them and stepped through. Ji Young's building was nicer than his due, no doubt, to her higher level. Her building had an elevator. It also had cameras posted in the corners of the ceiling. He bowed his head, hoped they wouldn't be able to pick up a clear image of him. Maybe they existed for resident security and nothing more. Or maybe other reasons. Maybe, just maybe, higher status invited more scrutiny. Should he remain a level three for the rest of his life? He'd never acquire a Cheetah 3000.

When Ji Young opened her door, she held her hands behind her back, perhaps hoping he hadn't seen them shake. She urged him into her apartment and scanned the hallway, as though she expected inspectors to crawl out of the walls and take the two of them in for evaluation. She shut the door and spoke in a hushed tone. "We'll have to wait until a bit later," she said. "This doctor, he doesn't start his practice until after midnight, until after the late show."

Teo plopped down on her couch. Ji Young's television dwarfed his. Covered half the wall. Reminded him of the screens in movie theaters, when they still existed. Ji Young joined him, sitting a few feet away. She picked up a bowl of half-eaten food. "You don't mind, do you?" She dipped a wooden spoon into the sludge and slurped it with her eyes clenched.

"Please," said Teo. The painkillers turned the couch into a boat swooping across wild waves. He focused on the television to keep from getting sick. Trudy and Matilda Minassian flew in a private airplane over a mountain range. Lush, apple-colored trees atop hillsides of rocks and snow. He'd wanted to visit Yosemite before the war, wanted to see something beyond the concrete and buildings of Los Angeles. The war changed all that. The barbarians in the north occupied stunning land. Deserts dominated the south. Might have been beautiful as well, but Teo never had the time nor the credits required to book a transport out of the city to see for himself.

"Same scenery, different sisters." Ji Young nodded at the television.

"Are you sure?" said Teo. "I thought Trudy and Matilda explored the dried-out waterfalls in Canada last week."

"Last week, the new Suzanne and Wilma explored this same range. I think it's somewhere in Washington. Or maybe Idaho. I don't even know if those borders exist anymore." She finished her dinner.

Teo got used to the increased effects of the medicine. He sunk into the couch and let his arm flop near Ji Young's thigh. He remembered the night they'd undressed. He'd commented on a tattoo drawn inside her leg. A bobcat.

Prowling. She'd refused to tell him where or why she'd had the colorful image carved into her flesh.

She must have noticed him staring at her. She cleared her throat. "I'm not going through that humiliation, Teo. Not a second time."

So negative. "What are you talking about?" He felt his head swivel on his neck. Had he smiled, for real? How long would he maintain the lie that he had no interest in trying procreation with her again? Nagging thoughts. Thoughts about what *could have been*. A waste of sorrow. The past could not be changed. The psychiatrists had fixed him so he could never recreate the night he'd spent with Ji Young and, this time around, give her what they both wanted.

Making love.

Yes, that's what the old timers called it, before the war. *Love.*

What did those sanctioned to procreate call it? Did they even know each other's names? Though he couldn't explain why, Teo figured mandated unions left participants drab, empty. Quick climax, no doubt. Then, like coming down off medicine briefly stimulating the heart, an emotional crash. He must have experienced it himself, though he could not recall when.

"I wish things were different between us." Had the painkillers prevented him from thinking before speaking?

His boss straightened her back. "Well, they're not. Things are the same and, no matter what happens with the doctor tonight, things will remain the same. Between you and me, that is."

"Don't you think about it?"

She stared at the scenery on the television the way Teo wished she'd stare at him.

SAME SONG, DIFFERENT BEAT

Teo stayed awake for the entire late show. Hubert Minassian interviewed his daughters Matilda and Suzanne. Same interview, different daughters. Suzanne sang a lounge version of "Sunshine Manifesto" with a small orchestra seated to the side of the stage. The latest actress to portray Suzanne had a nicer voice than the one who'd played her last week. She didn't move in quite the way the previous Suzanne had; last week's Suzanne snaked her body as she performed. She'd stirred Teo's useless desire. This week's Suzanne stood still, maintained a serious, business-like expression on her face. When the program concluded and the television shut itself off, Teo tapped Ji Young's ankle. She'd curled into a ball at the other end of the couch and rested her head on her hands. The pills wore off. The ringing returned, journeyed Teo's nerves, promised to become a nuisance. Ji Young sat up. She glanced at the TV, saw it had retired for the evening. She stood and said, "Let's go."

They crept through the streets, dodged rats and coyotes. The walk took forever. Teo said, "I need another pill." He imagined two tiny people with sledgehammers, each taking turns bashing their hammers into his temples. Like an old-fashioned clock, tick-tock, tick-tock, only very, *very* violent.

"I wouldn't," said Ji Young. "We don't know what the doctor's going to use to knock you out." Her legs moved with steady, confident precision. Gliding across the concrete. Teo considered arguing. A signal from the back of his mind, from the past, suggested he "be a man," a phrase indicating he not complain about pain, that he put up with the stress it caused and grit his teeth. Another dangerous belief from before the war. His father died from "being a man." A patrol officer for the Los Angeles Police Department, he'd tried to stop a young woman from jumping off a bridge spanning the L.A. River. As always, the river no more than a puddle. The

41

woman slipped while his father held her hand. They spilled over the side. The resulting gore from their impact with the concrete left little to place in the casket. They draped an American flag across his coffin. Several officers in uniform fired rifles. His superior gave a speech. He said his father had been a hero, a "*real* man." Teo wanted to explain how a simple glance at the apparatus between one's legs determined biological status. This sort of communication—humor, it used to be called—had already gone out of style. The war cemented the death of *genuine* laughter.

The ringing in his ear subsided as the lengthy walk to the Hollywood Hills burned the muscles in his legs and conjured natural, pain-killing dopamine. They marched up Beechwood, a winding road north of Franklin. Wealthier folks lived there before the war. They'd fled when the fighting started. No doubt they feared their selfish lifestyles wouldn't jibe with the Mutual Organization. In a red-bricked, one-story bungalow just below the dirt trail leading into the actual hills, a deep, amber light burned from a room within. Faint hints of the moon reflected off panels nailed to the roof in a haphazard manner. Obviously installed without the guidance of Mutual Construction.

"This is it." Ji Young held still as two coyotes trotted across the street. She knocked twice on a porch door on the side of the house. She counted, out loud, to five, and knocked three more times.

A white-haired man emerged from inside. Green scrubs. The kind Teo saw in hospitals before the war. Pink and crimson gore stained his clothes and his hands. He wiped his fingers with a paper towel. "Who is it?"

Ji Young announced herself. "My friend, he has one of those things in his head." The doctor looked older in the dim light. Ji Young introduced him as Dr. Pham. "This is Teo," she said.

"Another veteran?" said Dr. Pham.

"That's correct," said Teo.

The doctor shook his head. "Will he have the credits to cover the operation?"

"I added time to his badge." Ji Young winked at Teo.

Dr. Pham clicked his tongue. "I hope you feel the risk is worth it."

Ji Young urged Teo to follow her. He negotiated crumbling brick steps leading inside. He stood in a vast room with hardwood floors. Rusted medical instruments populated plastic pushcarts bordering a metal operating table. Crusty, maroon spots dotted it. The doctor handed Ji Young a reader to swipe Teo's badge. She took Teo's badge from his coverall without asking and ran it through the handheld machine. If she'd been able to add credits on her own, why hadn't she helped him save for the Cheetah 3000?

The doctor said, "Has he had any Mutual drugs in the last two hours?"

"No." Teo answered for himself.

This seemed to please the doctor. He nodded to the table. "Hop on up there, young man. Let's get your brain working properly again, how about it?"

Teo stretched out on the cold metal, stared at the flaking paint on the ceiling. A lone, fading bulb hung from a wire, provided the only light. "I hope your eyes are working properly." He clamped his hand over his mouth.

Laughing, the doctor said, "It's okay, son." He pulled on a pair of used rubber gloves and rummaged through several canisters on a cart to the left. "In *this* house, the revolution never happened. In *this* house, people are allowed to experience the full spectrum of emotions." He turned a knob on a canister with a facemask attached to it. He placed it over Teo's face and said, "Now, I want you to breathe deeply and count backwards."

Teo Paz, barely twenty years old, sat in a classroom in Franklin Hall at Los Angeles Community College. Two of his professors, Richard King, who, for some reason, insisted on being called Rafael, and Sandra Lorca, recruited students they considered ready for combat. They explained the revolution would take place soon. The 2036 elections satisfied no one and the state government in the north had proposed several bills intended to defund public institutions, including all community colleges. The local political leaders, including the city's mayor, Christian Santiago, called for secession from the north. Professor King, standing no taller than five feet, paced the front of the classroom, his hands behind his back, save for the occasional moment he'd bring them forward to move one side of his Van Dyke mustache out of his mouth. He said, "The north is aware we're preparing articles of secession. They've stationed the National Guard in Santa Barbara. Friendlies in the area are holding them back for the moment."

Professor Lorca jumped in—"Our primary obstacles, at this point, are our neighbors, families, and loved ones who refuse to go along with us. They are, understandably, afraid. But we cannot allow the fascists in Sacramento to determine our fates. Dying to protect all we've built here in Los Angeles is far more noble than allowing the bureaucrats to step in and dismantle the protections we've provided for the disadvantaged."

"Barring a miracle," said Professor King, "wherein the working schmucks figure it out on their own, our only option is to wait for an instigating gesture by the north."

Professor Lorca grinned. "Here's the good news…"

Teo woke up on the metal table in Dr. Pham's operating room. His head throbbed worse than before, though this pain seemed different. Natural. He ran his hand across the left side of his scalp. Stitches sealed a gash behind his ear. Dr. Pham said, "Ah, here he comes."

Ji Young hovered near Teo's feet. "How do you feel?"

The doctor prepared a syringe with a murky, black substance. He explained it would help with the discomfort and injected it into Teo's arm. He placed the needle on a tray and held up a small, silver cylinder splattered with blood. "This has been your master." He turned it around several times so Teo could see all sides of it. "The Mutual Organization has been watching you for some time. Maybe even since the war. Why? Who knows? You should begin recovering memories." He twisted a tiny dial on the cylinder. "This is the volume knob. They controlled it remotely. This means, if, as Ji Young has told me, the ringing in your ear increased over the last few days, you've done or said something that has alarmed them." He leaned closer. "You must be very careful. The Mutual Organization can do *unthinkable* things."

The drug swam through Teo's body. Relaxed him. Everything the doctor said didn't register as important. Gazing at Ji Young seemed, right then, much more pleasant than fussing over unseen officials tampering with his life.

Outside, the sun painted the hillside harsh orange. As Ji Young helped Teo off the table, the doctor said, "I would recommend catching a transport as soon as possible. This young man needs to rest."

More missed work. More lost credits.

"The walk down the hill will be taxing enough," said the doctor. "And when you're on the bus, avoid eye contact with anyone. If they ask about the stitches, just tell them he fell in his apartment." He grabbed Ji Young's wrist. "Under no circumstances do you let them know who operated on him."

"My memory is fine," said Ji Young. "You tell me this every time."

She draped Teo's arm around her shoulder and guided him out of the house and onto the sloped, winding road. The drug turned Teo's head into a top spin. He wanted to sleep. For a long, long time. Ji Young said, "Keep going." They walked in synch down the hill, nearly tumbling over several times. Ji Young caught him with each misstep and grunted as she forced him to regain his equilibrium. They mixed in with a crowd of workers waiting for a transport at Franklin and Bronson. She spoke into his unmolested ear— "Remember to smile."

They boarded a bus and sat near the back. Teo stared at the ruins of Hollywood, the collapsed pagoda of the Chinese Theater, the hollowed-out Kodak, the charred rubble of the Masonic lodge and El Capitan. Every star on the Walk of Fame had been sledgehammered and, per orders of the Mutual Organization, no one had cleaned the debris. They believed it important to remember the decadence from the old world, to make sure South California never catered to the whims of the few, the elite, ever again. A word rose from the opened vaults in Teo's mind:

Hypocrisy.

The society created by the Mutual Organization didn't seem very different from the old world. More streamlined, more honest, in some ways. In the old world, there had been many celebrities the working people paid attention to in effort to ignore their own, futile stations in life. There had been many songs, many television programs. They were all as equally pointless as the singular brand of entertainment provided by the Mutual Organization. For what had the war been fought?

A dangerous question.

He knew to keep it to himself. He looked at Ji Young. The morning sun cast a deep, red border around her. Almost like a halo. How long had this woman kept her opposition to the Mutual Organization to herself? She'd been lucky enough, apparently, to avoid service in the war. And she'd been, he assumed, smart enough to guard her opinions, to play the role…Then he remembered, she'd been a level seven at one point. He'd never witnessed a demotion. What did it look like?

Where were these questions coming from? Was he thinking? Doing precisely what he'd been told not to?

Ji Young walked with him to his apartment. She helped him up the stairs and swiped his badge at his door and led him to his couch. He held onto her arms as he lowered himself onto the cushions. Feeling her skin, heat rising from her flesh, something stirred within him. He tried to place his hands around the back of her head and bring her closer. He wanted to press his lips against hers, melt the ice lingering between them since the night he'd failed her. She resisted. He refused to let go. Finally, she slapped him on the side of his face that hadn't been sliced open.

Teo said, "I bet you anything, we can do it now. I bet that thing in my jaw controlled…"

"No," she said. "I wish we could be together that way, Teo, but now, now I'm going to need you to pretend we've never spoken, never met, outside of the market. You're just another employee. Almost anonymous." She handed him his badge and told him to take the day off. "I'll recover your credits. Then, that's it. You and I can never say anything other than amazing and wonderful to each other. I hope you understand."

She left.

Teo wanted to turn on the television, allow the noise and nonsense of Mutual entertainment to distract him. No programming existed during the day, however. This encouraged all members of the community to go to work. He swallowed a painkiller from the prescription Dr. Ortega had written him and fell asleep.

The fighting hadn't started in Los Angeles. Rich folks west of La Brea had too much to lose. Self-professed intellectuals claiming concern for the workers, the displaced, the marginalized, even they exhibited cowardice. Refused to pick up arms and kill the barbarians from the north. According to Teo's professors, the invading army, the erroneously named National Guard, had plans to move on Santa Barbara. No matter how many times Professor King argued with pundits on local television stations, he could not convince the population to procure weapons.

In a conference with Teo in his office on the LACC campus, Professor King revealed a plan to wake the south. He gave Teo a disposable cell phone, a piece of technology banned following the war, and told him to make his way to Santa Barbara and await instructions. For reasons Teo didn't understand, he obliged the professor. Didn't even question him. As though he'd been programmed, like a machine.

By 2028, an international police force monitored all transit, public and private. One could not board a bus, train, plane, or even a taxi without showing identification. An earlier, dubious plague excused this oppression. The obedient nodded, told puppet journalists they agreed liberty should come second to security. Destructive ad hominem greeted those who challenged the official narrative:

You're nothing but a conspiracy theorist!
You must be in cahoots with the Russians!
Domestic terrorist, how dare you!
Stop resisting progress!

The word progress, of course, used in an ironic manner, considering any movement toward voluntary servitude represented a step *backward.*

Teo navigated the road on foot. He'd taken apart an outlawed AR-15 given to him by the faculty of LACC and placed it under his toiletries in a cloth backpack. He wore faded blue jeans and a white T-shirt, blended in with migrants traveling from one farm to another. As long as he appeared dirty and poor, authorities watching checkpoints along the highway paid no attention.

It took him four days to reach the beautiful, seaside city. Spanish architecture glowed under the furious sun. He ducked into a restroom in an abandoned visitor's center on the edge of town. The toilets had been ripped from the walls and rats the size of cats skipped in and out of holes where the plumbing had been disrupted. He dialed a number Professor King provided. An electronic, modulated voice explained his mission:

"You are to survey the mayor's mansion and figure out the best way and time to assassinate her."

Mayor Karin Martinez had, as far as Teo knew, no enemies. She'd done her best to negotiate with forces from the north. She'd kept peace between the regions, insisting war provided no answers to the problems facing both parties. A self-described classical liberal, she believed all opinions should be heard, all options considered. She was also beautiful, which meant something to Teo, who'd had a crush on her since she'd upset the incumbent in 2034. She dressed a bit like a secret service agent in a tight, navy skirt and pale, button-down blouse. She never put her long, black hair into a ponytail, just let it flow around her shoulders while she sat at meetings with men and women who appeared so serious Teo wondered if they ate tar for breakfast and could not, thus, properly digest their food. Upon hearing his assignment, he called Professor Lorca to protest.

"I can't shoot a woman," he said.

The professor's first tactic had been to appeal to Teo's desire to abide by the social mores of the day—"Why is a woman politician any different from a male politician?" she said. "You're not a misogynist, are you?"

"Of course not." He'd have faced a firing line himself, should it ever be determined he harbored *any* bigotry of *any* kind.

Having failed to sway him through guilt, the professor tried an alternate route, she tried the truth—"The working class is complacent," she said. "They have video games, smartphones, movies, television, repetitive music that short-circuits the time and space in their minds they'd normally appropriate for critical inquiry. They must be *jarred* to action. Our friends in the media will blame the north for the assassination. The masses will be enraged and finally, we pray, grab hold of guns and avenge the death of Mayor Martinez."

Teo said he understood the strategy. "Why can't we choose a different tactic? The next in charge is Enrique Cortez. He's a fat slob no one will cry over."

"Exactly," said Professor Lorca. "Which is why a bullet to the head of precious, lovely Karin Martinez will jolt the sleeping proletariat to arms."

Teo said, "Aren't we, then, relying on latent sexism to accomplish our…"

Professor Lorca interrupted him—"Cheetah."

51

A cloud swirled through Teo's mind, vanquished his previous thoughts. "What did you say?"

"Cheetah." The professor cleared her throat before continuing. "You will stalk and murder Mayor Martinez, is that understood?"

His throat dried. His first effort to form words crashed on mountains of cotton. He swallowed, dredged saliva, and said, "Yes, ma'am."

Teo's head felt as though someone had loaded it with bricks. Normally, he would have dismissed the narrative he'd witnessed while sleeping as a dream. But he knew better. He knew what unfolded had been a memory. His jaw hurt where the doctor had carved into it. He tried grinding his teeth. Shockwaves tore through his skull. Nothing like the pain caused by the gadget the doctor removed, however.

What else could he now remember about the war? He'd gone through with his mission. He'd spied on Karin Martinez for three nights, watching her from a hill on the backside of her mansion. She often retreated to her bedroom on the third floor and, removing her skirt and blouse, danced in her underwear to mambo music played loud enough for Teo to hear from his perch. Her way of easing stress, he assumed. His libido functioned in those days and raw instincts suggested he scale the tangerine walls of the elaborate villa, crawl through the mayor's open window, strip down to his shorts, and dance right along with her. Any time he questioned his orders, however, his professor's voice bulldozed his thoughts—"Cheetah"—and his resolve to murder Karin Martinez returned.

He shot her on the third night. She'd swayed in front of her window, the straps on her wine-red bra sliding down her shoulders. Celia Cruz's voice echoed through the valley. The mayor must have had one heck of a sound system, more of that extravagant technology people in the old world had been so easily distracted by; Teo put the back of the mayor's head in a rather cheap sight on the AR-15. He focused on the center of her wavy, black hair, and squeezed the trigger. Somewhere, he could not recall, he'd been trained with the firearm. He let the bullet fly with confidence, barely taking time to line up the shot in the shabby scope. Backsplash painted the mayor's bedroom window frame a bright, scarlet hue. The woman collapsed.

Teo fled in the darkness. He disassembled the gun and left it scattered between Los Angeles and Santa Barbara. Local authorities had been preoccupied with the army gathering on the north side of the city. The mayor's security didn't realize what had happened until the next morning, when the mayor's lone servant entered her bedroom with a tray of bacon and eggs. By that time, Teo had reached Ventura. He ducked into a motel, paid cash for the privilege of checking in anonymously. On the television which, in those days, recklessly allowed viewers a variety of choices and channels, newscasters parroted the official story: Someone from the north assassinated Santa Barbara's beloved matriarch. Interviews conducted with people on the streets of Los Angeles presented an angry population ready to overdose on vengeance:

This is the last straw, let me tell you.

They call us snowflakes? Well, my friend, you've summoned a blizzard.

If those animals think they can intimidate us, they're in for a sore surprise.

Teo wondered why it would take the murder of an innocent to conjure such passion. Anger with the north, and the rest of the country, for that matter, had boiled for years.

How tragic that a woman with peace in her heart should have to die to stir the lazy masses.

The war started, officially, a week later, when a militia from the south marched to Santa Barbara and engaged the National Guard in a firefight. Professor King posted Teo on the roof of a high rise in MacArthur Park. When clusters of soldiers from the north got through the other barriers between L.A. and Santa Barbara, Teo and his comrades picked them off, leaving stacks of dead, blood-soaked bodies in the streets of the Rampart district. Fighting lasted for two years before Professor King met with delegates from the north to fashion a truce.

All soldiers who fought for the south were put through psychiatric evaluations. For reasons Teo couldn't remember, he'd agreed to start in the new society on the bottom, at level one, sifting through the newly formed garbage heap for recyclable items careless citizens tossed out with their regular trash.

"Why in the world would I ever go for that?" he said to his empty apartment. He put his hand over his mouth, realizing, perhaps, his apartment might not be empty. Not at all.

Memories of the war, the carnage, disemboweled soldiers, corpses with missing limbs, decapitated bodies, rats and coyotes feasting on wasted flesh in the streets, made it impossible for Teo to eat breakfast. Whether awake or asleep, the horrific products of armed conflict dominated his thoughts. As he struggled to push them away, to find anything in his mind to replace macabre reels playing over and over, like Mutual television without the relief of different actors performing the same roles, only one thought seemed powerful enough to quell the flashbacks: a manufactured impression of a *real* cheetah, running through the wild. In deeper sleep, Teo identified with the cheetah, believed he, in fact, *was* the cheetah, running, running, running. His concept of a jungle had been created by movies viewed on televisions and computer screens before the war. When exhaustion caught up with him, his brain nudged him toward a waking state. He then found himself running *from* the cheetah. He couldn't see it, he simply understood it existed just beyond his vision, and if he didn't keep moving, if he didn't wake up, the cheetah would catch him, and that would be that.

On the transport to the market, he ignored a half dozen men and women in gray coveralls, distributed evenly throughout the bus. He'd put a bandage over the scar on the back of his cheek and swallowed several painkillers. The need to unload his conscience simmered under his skin. He'd played such a significant role in the war. Who'd programmed him to forget it? Who'd decided he should not be allowed to negotiate his own moral constitution? He couldn't believe these questions even existed. As he stood in the parking lot of the market, he waited for Ji Young, hoping he could isolate her and tell her what he'd learned. Makiko, dressed in a violet coverall, her lips painted the same, approached. "Your troubles are over?" she said.

He pointed to the bandage on the side of his face. "Yes."

The young woman's eyes danced in circles. "Goodness," she said. "That looks like an amazing amount of trouble."

"Indeed." He smiled. "But I'm better now. In fact, I feel wonderful, amazing." Angels lifted the corners of his mouth to manufacture a smile. He would not give this woman any reason to suspect he'd wandered into the swamps of negativity.

Thought. You mean thought.

"That's wonderful," she said. "Amazing, really."

"It is amazing." He wanted to pat her on her shoulder, a gesture from before the war signifying camaraderie the Mutual Organization no longer deemed appropriate.

An inspector, an older man whose white roots betrayed the brown dye in his hair, arrived and announced, "Your manager is having troubles today. I'll attend to her duties until she returns." He opened the door and greeted the workers, one by one, as they entered, "A wonderful, amazing morning, yes?" His badge introduced him as Hugo Nespa. On the photograph on his badge, a younger Hugo Nespa sported long, dark hair and round spectacles, the kind worn by many of Teo's professors at LACC.

The workers responded, "Wonderful, wonderful, amazing morning."

As Teo entered the building, the inspector angled himself in front of him to slow him down. He glanced at Teo's badge and said, "Wonderful morning?"

"Amazingly wonderful," said Teo.

The inspector smiled and stepped out of his way. "A freethinker. Interesting."

Teo followed Miguel to the stockroom. Miguel stood near a sink and scrubbed at a stain of what appeared to be dried breakfast powder on his diesel coverall. He spoke as he cleaned his uniform. "You see the latest ad for the Panther 3000?"

Teo grabbed the bridge of his nose and squeezed. "Pretty sure it's called a Cheetah 3000."

A small patch of beard grew just under the middle of Miguel's lower lip. As he approached the clipboard with the day's assignments on it, he said, "Sometimes, Teo, sometimes…" He tapped the clipboard twice and began stocking lavender boxes of dessert mix into a shopping cart.

As Teo replaced amber boxes of vegetable powder with maize-colored boxes, he listened to the radio overhead.

"Sunshine Manifesto" finished. The DJ announced, "How wonderful is that? The latest version of 'Sunshine Manifesto' is amazing, I'm sure you agree. Just to be safe, let's revisit the version produced just before this one." He then played *the very same song*. No doubt, at that point. Teo paid strict attention, counting the number of beats per minute—123. Both songs. No difference in the instrumentation, the voices, the location of the verses and chorus and bridge. All identical. His hands trembled. He *needed* to tell someone. He glanced at the front counter, where Ji Young should have been standing. The inspector, Hugo Nespa, rested his elbow on the black, plastic frame of the credit-reducing machine's screen. He nodded at Teo and smiled. Not a friendly smile, rather, the smile of a man aware he knew far more than anyone else in the building.

Teo stopped pretending he didn't understand what had happened. He remembered the boot camp, run by his professors. They'd tampered with his mind. How, he didn't know. He remembered being a student interested in changing the system from the inside-out for most of his college career. Then, as if by magic, he'd become a revolutionary. Professor Lorca spent hours with him, talking to him, convincing him he'd been victimized by the barbarians from the north who wanted the south to follow their strict, oppressive rules. He'd fought in the civil war believing the result would be freedom. As he stacked boxes of vegetable powder, as he realized how pointless life had become, as he honored his inability to shout out his certainty that the entertainment the Mutual Organization provided never changed, never offered anything new, interesting, mentally stimulating, he recognized the revolution had been a failure. And his role in making it happen, the killing of a reasonable politician, had left the foulest stench on his conscience. He looked at his hands. The image of a cheetah, bearing down on him, charged through his mind. His dreams before the removal of the chip in his jaw, his dreams of fleeing something he couldn't escape, had been about the cheetah, he just hadn't been able to see it. He recalled a psychology class in which the professor suggested dreams were memories, filed away for unconscious keeping. But he'd never seen a cheetah, not in real life. Zoos had been outlawed long before the civil war. The only animals left in the wild? Rats and coyotes.

Lunchtime arrived. Teo sat next to Miguel. He believed Miguel the only person in the market he could possibly trust. Makiko droned on about the Minassian sisters' appearance on the Late Show the night before; Teo wanted to scream at her, he wanted to say, "Wake up!" But he felt certain she'd already gotten him in trouble with the inspector a few days earlier, when he'd first noticed the music provided by the Mutual Organization might be the same song, played over and over. She asked him what he thought of the Minassian sisters. He said, "They're amazing, wonderful."

"Yes, yes." She nearly choked on her food powder trying to speak and eat at the same time. "They are. They're wonderful and amazing and I think that's just amazing and wonderful." She distributed expectant eyes to everyone at the table.

Did she...?

Did she work *directly* for the Mutual Organization? A full-fledged spy?

Teo's colleagues chimed in, each offering a variation of, "Yes, amazing, wonderful," or, "Yes, wonderful, amazing."

Miguel spoke with a hint of resentment, his voice refusing to echo the forced joy and exuberance the other staff displayed. Teo waited for the lunchroom to clear out. As Miguel finished his sludge, scraped the sides of his bowl, wincing as he shoved the last bits into his mouth, he started to get up. Teo grabbed the sleeve on his uniform. "Can I talk to you for a minute?"

"Make it quick."

Teo set down his spoon, having barely touched the slop in his bowl. "You fought in the war, yes?"

Miguel didn't look at him. "That's what they tell me." He held up his ID badge. The photograph on it had been taken before he'd grown his mustache and the scant patch of beard clinging to his chin. Underneath the orange L3, his badge carried the same symbol Teo's did: two guns crossed like bones beneath a rainbow-colored skull. This signified veteran status.

"What do you remember about it?"

Smiling, Miguel said, "Amazingly, wonderfully, not a gosh darned thing."

"Do you remember how it started?"

"Nope."

"Listen," said Teo. "We fought in that war to get rid of tyranny."

"True." Miguel nodded, his smile widening. "And what an amazing job we did."

"I remember the world being imperfect, but we had choices, before the war. We had *choices*, Miguel."

Miguel's attitude changed. He sighed and rested his elbows on the table.

"You realize," said Teo, "that *we* fired the shot that killed Mayor Martinez."

"I don't…I don't understand."

Teo moved closer, spoke so no one else could hear him. "I killed her, Miguel. That's how I know. The civil war started because of a *lie*."

"You sound awfully negative, my friend." Miguel leaned away from him.

"Cut that...*shit* out," said Teo. "The Mutual Organization claim they liberated us. The *opposite* has happened, don't you see?"

His coworker didn't flinch at the banned word. He pointed to his mustache and miniscule beard. "If we're so oppressed," he said, "why hasn't the Mutual Organization told me to shave?"

Insane. Teo had no idea how to respond.

"Yeah." Miguel nodded, this time confident he'd made his point beyond any possible rebuttal. "The only thing I'm interested in is finally getting ahead credit-wise so I can buy a Panther 3000."

Without thinking about it, Teo said, "You mean a *Cheetah* 3000."

Miguel jabbed him with his elbow. "I don't want you talking to me anymore."

Hugo Nespa poked his head in the door. "Gentlemen? It's time for recess, isn't it?"

Teo spent the rest of the afternoon forcing himself not to think. Miguel walked near the inspector during recess and spoke to him quietly. They eyed Teo during their discussion. Didn't even hide it. Makiko marched next to Teo, asking him who he thought would play Trudy Minassian next week. "I don't know," he said to her. "It's usually a surprise, isn't it?" He wondered, however, whether the shifting Minassians were really the same people, like the song, "Sunshine Manifesto," pretending to be different from week to week. He wondered, also, whether everyone had a chip implanted in their jaw bones. Miguel never complained of headaches. Then again, Miguel had proven himself a traitor. Had he spoken to the previous inspector, Claude Ramirez, about Teo's concern—his, now, *justified* concern—over the similarity of the alleged multiple versions of "Sunshine Manifesto"? Had Teo put the blame on Makiko for no reason? He wanted to apologize to her, but that would have confused her, compelled questions that might, ultimately, lead her to betraying him after all.

No inspectors observed him on the transport he rode to his apartment. Another word stored away in the box of taboo terminology dusted itself off and presented itself as he considered the possibility the results of the operation had caused him to overthink: *Paranoia*. This term had been applied to anyone who questioned the revolution before the civil war. When he arrived home, the lack of obvious tampering in his apartment reinforced his suspicion that he'd fabricated his persecution. The cushions on his couch had not been flipped over. He turned on the television without any issues. Wilma Minassian's familiar face filled the screen. She cast the usual aspersions on the barbarians in the north—"Reports from Old San Fran suggest the fascists are now separating children from their families and cooking and serving the children as ice cream to foreign dignitaries." Must have been Saturday. The cannibalism story always ran on Saturdays.

Comfortable he had nothing to worry about, Teo boiled water and poured it over a bowl filled with equal parts meat and vegetable powder. He sat on his couch and scooped the sludge into his mouth. The news broadcast gave way to a variety hour with the entire Minassian clan. They sang renditions of "Sunshine Manifesto," renditions that actually differed from each other. First a reggae version, then a lounge version, and a rousing finale of the techno version the radio played on the transport and at the market. During the finale, the black, plastic frame of the television screen bubbled, as though it had been heated to a dangerous temperature. Teo squinted. The colors on the screen blended like various shades of paint, swirling in a bucket. He sniffed the air, thinking, perhaps, his apartment had been gassed. This would be the last thing he would remember about the evening.

Teo's legs dangled over the end of the couch when he awoke the next morning. He thought little of it as a different kind of headache nagged. He imagined microscopic level one workers swinging sledgehammers against his brain pan at a quick, steady rhythm, similar to the chug-a-chug of the old blue line subway from downtown Los Angeles to Long Beach. He felt the side of his face, for the surgery scar. It had healed overnight. Or disappeared. This should have concerned him. As he sat up, however, the altered dimensions of his couch hogged his attention. Someone had snuck into his apartment while he slept and replaced it with a smaller couch. Same flower and vine pattern, same milky shade of beige in the background. Just shorter. He examined the cushions. Also smaller. He scanned his apartment and realized everything, in fact, had shrunk—his television, his coffee table, his entire kitchen. Even the ceiling had lowered. He peered out the window over the sink. The position of his apartment within the city had changed as well. The decadent, bullet-ridden Hollywood sign no longer lurked in the haze over the hills to the north. Logic settled amidst his confusion, insisted he accept he'd been moved during his slumber.

He thought back to the previous evening. He remembered eating dinner and watching television. Then, nothing. No recollection of anything, not even laying down to go to sleep. That demon from the old world, paranoia, suggested he'd been drugged somehow. His food? He opened the cabinets over his stove. Corn-colored boxes of powdered food instead of the pumpkin-colored boxes he preferred. He called out, "Hello?" The apartment he'd been placed in did not even have a separate bathroom. A basin beneath a faucet and a toilet occupied the corner opposite the kitchen. The proper tenant, obviously, a level one. He left the strange apartment for the street.

The Hollywood Hills lay far to the west. He'd been relocated to Highland Park. He weaved through side streets until he found Figueroa. The old shops on the main road had been boarded up. Much fighting in the civil war took place there and the area hadn't recovered. He stood among a crowd of level ones at a designated stop for a transport headed toward downtown. The smiles on their faces—transparent, forced. The few who made eye contact showed no signs of happiness. He'd felt the same when he'd been a level one, after the war, sifting through decaying items on the garbage heap. Putrid odors seeped into the nostrils like invaders, staining the senses with such tenacity the weekends did little to subdue them. Misery, an aspect of life the civil war promised to vanquish, had gone nowhere.

Throngs of people filled the transport. Teo stood amidst workers in dull, fading coveralls. Most of them reeked of rotting corpses. As the bus rumbled across Figueroa and zig-zagged toward Wilshire, he listened for conversations, for the usual exchanges of *wonderful* and *amazing*. Aside from the hiss and grinding of the transport's motor, the only other sound on the bus came from the speakers. A stripped-down version of "Sunshine Manifesto" pounded the air with heavy drums and bass and a woman with an angry voice not so much singing as *barking* the lyrics. The Minassian sisters' tincture for the ears transformed into a choppy, unappealing assault. Did nothing to ease his mind. Doubtful it brought peace to the other passengers.

He transferred to his normal route near Seventh Street. Less than half the people on the transport from Highland Park joined him. A Muzak version of "Sunshine Manifesto" dripped from the speakers like a sugar-heavy syrup, the kind Teo smothered pancakes in before powdered food became the only legal sustenance. The sun painted the floor and seats of the bus butterscotch hues. Two passengers resembled inspectors, but they seemed preoccupied with their own thoughts, never once glancing Teo's way. He watched them as he stepped off the transport in his neighborhood. He walked against the flow of people headed toward the bus stop. As soon as he splashed water on his face and changed into a new coverall, he'd join them.

He managed to catch the front door to his building as a woman he didn't recognize hurried out, wiping remnants of breakfast powder from the sides of her mouth. He climbed the stairs to his floor, dodging more people he'd never seen before, all in a hurry. At his apartment, he swiped his ID badge and tried to turn the handle. The scanner cawed like an ancient crow with something caught in its throat. The handle refused to budge. He tried again. Same results. Finally, he looked at his badge, considered the possibility the chip on it had worn down. The picture on the badge had not changed. The name and level, however, had. According to the badge, he was Thiago Puga, a level one. He beat on the door. Nobody answered. He shouted. He said, "Let me in my…" He almost said *goddamn*. In a calmer voice, he said, "Please, let me in." No one responded. He examined his badge again. Had his kidnappers played a joke on him?

He descended the steps. He exited through a rear door in the lobby and approached the management office, run by an older man named Mr. Park. Mr. Park had given up on his thinning hairline long ago and shaved his scalp bald. Age had manufactured welts above and below his eyes. When Teo stepped into the office, a different man, a younger man, sat at Mr. Park's desk.

Teo said, "Where is Mr. Park?"

The younger man nodded his round, cherub face. "How can I help you?"

"I'm looking for Mr. Park."

The younger man said, "Yes. I am Mr. Park. How can I help you?"

"I'm sorry," said Teo. "I meant the other Mr. Park, the one who normally works here."

"I am the only Mr. Park employed here. Can I help you with something?"

Teo considered arguing the matter further. He asked himself what that would accomplish. "I can't get into my apartment."

"Ah, no problem." The younger man stood. He'd spilled ink on his hands and decided to wipe his fingers on the sides of his crimson coveralls. "Which apartment do you live in?" He reached for a clipboard hanging on a wall near the door.

"Second floor," said Teo. "Two-seventeen."

The younger man flipped through sheets of paper on the clipboard. He found whatever he'd sought and said, "No, sir. That apartment belongs to Teo Paz." He put the clipboard back on the wall. "Perhaps you have the wrong building." He sat down again.

"No, no," said Teo. "*I'm* Teo Paz." He gestured toward his ID.

The younger man squinted and read the name on the badge. "Says you're Thiago Puga. Level one. You definitely don't live here." A grin washed across the younger man's face.

Teo nodded and backed out of the office. "Amazing. I've made an amazing mistake."

"I'm glad you see it that way." The younger man stood once more. "Have a wonderful, amazing morning."

"Yes," said Teo. "Wonderful. Amazing." He walked to the bus stop. Rode a transport to the market. If Ji Young had returned, she would no doubt want to learn about everything that had happened. As the bus rumbled and rocked across the unkempt roads, Teo fantasized walking into the market and finding his ID badge, the correct badge, waiting for him. He'd discover he'd accidentally taken someone else's badge. Of course, this made no sense, and the portion of his brain freed by the operation intruded, reminded him all the reasons such a scenario could not occur.

The market had already opened when he arrived. He should have been concerned about the credits he'd lose for his tardiness. For the moment, however, he no longer felt the need to worry about credit. A Cheetah 3000 authoring genuine happiness seemed absurd. Nobody outside the Mutual Organization owned a private vehicle. He almost never saw one on the street, so why had he spent so much energy chastising himself for not being able to save enough to purchase one?

He strolled through the door, he turned to the front desk, where a woman roughly the same age as Ji Young stood, cashing out a level five who'd loaded up on dessert powder. This woman wore a cherry red coverall. She'd painted her eyelids the same shade. She did not strike Teo as the type of person hired for inspection work. He waited for her to finish with the customer and stepped forward. "Is Ji Young still having troubles?"

The woman laughed. "Excuse me?"

"Ji Young," he said. "She had trouble yesterday. Didn't show for work."

"I'm sorry." The woman flipped her straight, black hair over the back of her shoulders. Her eyes projected the indignation Ji Young had the night Teo failed to perform in bed. She said, "I had no trouble yesterday. To be honest, your question is quite negative."

Teo glanced at her badge. The woman's picture sat above the name Ji Young and her level five designation. "I see," he said. "There must be some kind of mistake. You have the same name as the woman who normally runs this market."

"I think the mistaken one is you…" She leaned forward, obviously reading his badge. "T-yaw-go, is that how you pronounce it?"

He lifted his badge, looked at it upside down. "I don't know. This isn't me."

The woman craned to examine it again. "Looks just like you."

"I know that," said Teo. "My name is Teo, though. Teo Paz."

"Oh," she said. "We have a Teo Paz here as well." She pointed over his shoulder, down the aisle he normally worked. A man in a puce coverall stacked brown boxes of vegetable powder on the shelves. Teo walked away from the woman while she spoke. "If you have no intention of making a purchase," she said, "it would be amazing and wonderful if you left the premises."

Teo approached the man stacking vegetable powder. He must have resembled an alien, walking the Earth for the first time, as though he'd never seen the shelves of a grocery store before, as though he'd never watched someone else stock product, as though he'd never done the very same thing. The man noticed him and stopped.

"Hello, friend." The man looked nothing like him. A thick mess of curly hair clutched the top of his head like a sea creature holding on for dear life. Much, much lighter skin. He appeared to be several years younger than Teo. Young enough to have avoided fighting in the civil war. Teo read his badge. Indeed, it designated the man as a Teo Paz, and even had the symbol next to his level, indicating his veteran status.

"When did you start working here?" he said to the man.

"Excuse me, friend?"

Annoyed, he repeated the question.

"That is a wonderfully, amazingly personal question."

Contrary to the cheery, swing jazz rendition of "Sunshine Manifesto" dropping from the speakers in the ceiling like a light, pleasant rain, anger bloomed inside Teo's mind. In the war, he would have grabbed the imposter and slammed his head into the shelf until he told him the truth. A quick ride to Identity Adjustment would follow. The only thing keeping him and everyone else repeating the inane words, Amazing, Wonderful, over and over again. A million soldiers of rage jogged through his blood. He barely opened his mouth when he spoke. "Who *are* you?"

The man must have never encountered an angry human being. His thin smile remained intact. "What kind of question is that?"

"Answer me." Teo stepped up to the man, raised his chest, let him ponder the physics problem engaging his fury represented.

Even this, however, failed to impress the imposter. "I think you're having some troubles." He pointed to Teo's badge. "I think you don't even belong here."

Ah, the threat of calling on authority. Something Teo had fought in the civil war to eliminate. He backed off. "You're right," he said. "I apologize. I'm wonderfully, amazingly sorry."

The man huffed his chest. In the world before the war, that would have been an invitation to fight. "I should hope so."

Teo continued down the aisle, toward the stockroom. He looked for anyone he might recognize. Before reaching the door to the stockroom, he bumped into a diminutive woman in a scarlet coverall. He read the name on her badge, then grabbed her by her shoulders. "You're not Makiko." His forehead flushed as the rage he'd attempted to quell burst forth, planted the seeds for a new, refreshing kind of headache.

The woman pushed him away. Her eyes expanded, threatened to jump from her skull and flee in terror. "Ji Young!" She ran toward the front register.

Nothing Teo could do to appease her at that point. He pushed through the door to the stockroom. Several employees stood by the clipboard with the day's duties on it. He said, "I'm looking for Miguel."

One of the men, bone-skinny, his orange coverall draped over his shoulders like drooping curtains, stepped forward. "I'm Miguel. What can I do for you on this amazing, wonderful morning?"

Teo left the stockroom without saying anything. The walls and the ceiling shrank. He imagined everyone in the store mashed to liquid and bones, like refuse in a trash compactor. Breathing became a challenge. He needed to see the sky, even if the sun hid behind clouds of smog. He needed to feel wide open space. He hurried for the front door, nearly knocking over the imposter Teo.

Two inspectors, men twice as big as Teo, scrunched their massive bodies through the entrance. The woman claiming to be Ji Young spoke to them while pointing at Teo. "This is him."

Teo struggled to draw air into his lungs. The woman had done it. She'd called the....the *GODDAMN* authorities. He rested his palms on his knees, as though staring at the speckled tiles on the floor might quell panic sweeping through him, turning his heart into a jackhammer.

One of the inspectors, a man whose hands looked big enough to wrap around Teo's skull and shatter it with the slightest pinch, grabbed Teo by the collar of his coverall and forced him to stand straight.

The other inspector used a black, handheld scanner to swipe Teo's ID badge. He studied the data the machine returned and nodded. His eyebrows almost met at the bridge of his nose. Big, severe brows. Less like hair and more like bristles on a brush for animals with tough hides. "You're not where you're supposed to be, are you, Thiago?"

In the war, Teo would have fought his way out. He would have snatched the nearest piece of wood or metal, turned it into a weapon, and bashed at these giants until he shattered their bones and tore apart their muscles, left them weeping on those speckled, blood-stained tiles. But these were his people. They were not supposed to be enemies.

The inspector holding him by his collar dragged him toward the door.

The other inspector said, "Let's put you back in your proper place, shall we?"

Something clogged his breathing, as though someone had poured wet concrete down his throat. He tried to speak, but made no noise. He would not allow them to take him to Identity Adjustment. If he had to die trying to escape, so be it.

Each inspector took hold of one of his arms and led him through the parking lot to a white van with the Mutual Organization's logo—four clasped hands attached to crooked elbows, arranged in a circle—painted on the side of it. He bent his legs, picked up his feet to create more weight for the men abducting him. They adjusted their own efforts and carried him to the van. The doors opened from the inside and two more inspectors helped secure Teo to a bench seat.

Identity Adjustment occupied the old LACC campus, near Melrose and Vermont. The van did not head that way. Were they taking Teo someplace worse, someplace he would not live to remember? The van turned north on Van Ness. The garbage heap loomed over burned-out buildings surrounding the old cemetery. He finally spoke: "What amazing, wonderful plans do you have for me?"

The inspector in the passenger seat, the man with the severe eyebrows, said, "We're delivering you to your proper place of employment."

"Oh, no." Teo shook his head. "No, no, no. I'm telling you, I am *not* a level one."

The inspectors sitting on either side of him, both in dull, gray coveralls, grunted. They'd each grown sideburns so thick they looked like wings. The inspector to his left, streaks of white in his chestnut hair betraying his age, said, "That's an awfully negative way to look at things."

"No," said Teo. "I'm very proud of the fact that I worked my way up to the next level."

"Except you didn't." The badge worn by the inspector to his right indicated he too fought in the civil war. "You're clearly a level one and you should be grateful for what you have."

The horrid stench of decay wafted into the van as they neared the gates to the garbage heap. Nothing in the world smelled as bad as rotting flesh. Teo thought of the war, of running through the streets of the Rampart district, dodging bullets and bodies. The entire city had reeked of death. The longer the war continued, the more he'd considered suicide, just to escape the odor.

The driver pulled up to the gates. A level one greeted him, opened the chain-link fence surrounding the mountain. The driver parked near a shed at the base. Teo remembered the year after the war he'd spent taking a transport every morning, filing through the swinging gate for foot traffic, and prepping for the grueling climb to the top. His feet constantly sank in the muck as he followed his colleagues up a trail cutting through the moistened slop. They spent their day marching in a circle, downwards, piercing any objects that appeared recyclable, and dropping them into a cloth bag draped over their shoulders. He often mistook dried bones for wooden materials he thought could be refashioned and made useful once more. In those days, he mouthed a scream for half a minute upon waking in the morning, letting out air, like a leaking tire, unable to give his anger sound in fear of a neighbor reporting him for exhibiting negative behavior. The same urge he'd had during the war, the urge to end his life, gained momentum the longer he slaved on the trash heap. The day he'd been told of his promotion, he went home and turned up the volume on his television while he wept with joy.

He'd forgotten all that. The electronic device in his jaw had, it seemed, rendered both his long and short-term memories inactive. Information continued to be stored in his brain, but he didn't have access to it. As the doors to the van opened and an inspector clicked the belt securing Teo to the bench, Teo shoved him out of his way and ran for the fence. No one in the new world had weapons. That had been an agreement across the board. Being smaller in stature than the inspectors, he believed he could outpace them. His hands stung as his fingers clasped the mesh, metal diamonds. He scaled the fence like a salamander climbing a wall. The inspectors shouted, promised he'd be amazed by the wonderful, amazing penalties the Mutual Organization would level against him for his antisocial decisions. He no longer cared. He would *not* return to the trash heap. He wanted to explain to the inspectors, wanted to say, I'd rather be dead, but he ignored the ingrained need to justify his actions to others. Swinging his legs over the top of the fence, he let himself fall to the ground. Then he ran. He ran south, past Melrose, and cut left on Clinton. He navigated minor streets until he returned to his neighborhood. When he got to his building, he stopped near the curved walk leading to the front door. As he caught his breath, the front door opened and a flock of inspectors dressed in black coveralls emerged from the apartment complex. They carried something in their arms Teo had not seen since the war—weapons. They'd each been armed with rifles. From the abandoned parking lot to the side of the building, a box truck rolled out and into the street behind him. He did not see who spoke, he heard only a voice devoid of compassion say, "You were given a chance to comply. The choice is no longer yours to make."

He had no body. This made his position in the jungle ambiguous. Emerald and mahogany hues surrounded him. Locating his limbs or his torso proved impossible. The urge to dismiss this as a dream, to wake up, nagged. A bird adorned with brilliant, rose-colored feathers, a daffodil belly, and a beak like the clamp on a wrench, flew in front of him and landed on a tree. It squawked several prolonged warnings: "Run, now! Run, now!" The foliage rustled and a low growl disrupted the scene. Patient paws patted the ground, like an infant, taking steps in a sleeper on a carpeted floor. The eyes of the beast glowed through shadows created by a tapestry of leaves. He tried to run but could not train his mind to understand the concept without his body as a point of reference. The sleek, spotted cat leapt from the darkness. Black, symmetrical lines pointed to its eyes. His mind demanded he shriek, but he found no vocal cords, no throat through which air could negotiate.

A flash of light blinded him and he found himself in a bedroom filled with toys. Wooden bars imprisoned him. Two people, a man and a woman, shouted at each other. He could not see them. He struggled for a broader view of his cage. In the far corner, a stuffed cheetah with exaggerated eyes and a fabric tongue draped down the side of its grinning mouth, stared at him. He felt certain the man and woman arguing were doing so from *inside* the stuffed cheetah.

After the war, the lone thought lurking deepest in Teo Paz's conscious mind was: Never submit to another psychiatric evaluation. How much had he done for the revolution? The response of the doctors, the so-called experts on human behavior, had been to neuter him for fear of him creating a new generation of fighters. "Our world," said the woman who'd made the diagnosis, "cannot tolerate aggression of any kind."

He couldn't remember why he'd submitted to the treatment. They'd injected him with what they called a "vaccine to toxic masculinity." Despite feeling more desire to be with a woman than ever before, he could not maintain an aroused state for any significant time. The prospect of sex materialized, his body responded and as soon as he recognized the response, he reminded himself the Mutual Organization had sterilized him. His body would relax. His mind, however, would not. He'd been cheated, he knew it, and he could do nothing about it. If he spoke up, his colleagues or an inspector or a neighbor would have accused him of engaging in complaint. This would have provided the Mutual Organization an excuse to do even more damage.

He crossed his legs when the box truck he'd been thrown into turned onto Vermont and headed north, scattering anorexic rats in the road. The rodents struck Teo, right then, as the only creatures enjoying freedom. As the truck veered into the oval lot in the hollowed-out center of the former Los Angeles City College campus and parked, something tasting like bile ran down Teo's throat. He wanted to vomit. He had nothing in his stomach to throw up, but this did not stop him from developing a flu-like illness without the normal provocation of legitimate, air-born disease.

Two inspectors dressed in black, wearing mirrored sunglasses, a fashion accessory only the Minassians seemed to have use for since the war, escorted him, at gunpoint, into what had once been Jefferson Hall. A blue sign posted in the dead grass in front of the building announced Identity Adjustment. Teo humored himself, thought maybe the worst they could do would be to literally chop off his offensive genitalia. They rendered that part of his body useless anyway, why not just get rid of it? The inspectors checked him in at a chipped, wooden u-shaped front desk. A level seven shuffled papers and swiped the ID badge on Teo's chest. The clerk's square glasses rested too high on his nose, forcing him to constantly push them down with his pinky. He said, "Thiago Puga?"

An inspector nudged Teo's shoulder.

"That's not me," said Teo.

"Oh dear." The clerk assembled several documents with haste. To the inspectors, he said, "Any idea how long he's been deluded?"

Neither inspector answered. Both men thrust their shoulders and barrel chests outward, in exaggerated pride, as though this might be the only currency they carried in a world claiming no need for physical power. One grunted, just under his breath, a sure sign he had no idea what the clerk meant and felt sufficiently embarrassed by his ignorance. The other inspector said, "Just check him in."

The inspectors took the paperwork from the clerk and marched Teo down the hall. They led him to the old performing arts building which now, according to a plaque above the center door, served as Patient Quarters. They escorted him to a small room with a cot and an old school desk placed before a window no larger than the dimensions of an ancient book, the kind one held in one's hands when the state still allowed such things. Iron bars flanked the window on the inside and the outside. The inspectors placed a clipboard with the paperwork on a mounted hook outside.

They instructed Teo to relax as they closed and latched the door.

An orderly dressed in a white coverall delivered a bowl of powdered food a few hours later. Teo said, "Can you tell me what's going on?" The orderly shook her head.

"I only take care of the minor details." Her badge indicated level five.

"How can you be that high on the ladder and not know anything?"

"I see why they brought you here." She smiled and whisked her hand at the food, suggesting he hurry.

"I'm not hungry."

"You have to eat." She stood by the door. "My job is to see to it you don't do anything to hurt yourself."

"The only thing hurting me, right now," he said, "is the Mutual Organization."

The orderly—Flora Curadora, according to her badge—denounced his description of the situation. "You've proven yourself sick, beyond any normal troubles. The specialists here will put you back together."

"But I'm not broken," said Teo.

Flora pushed her slick, dark hair above her ear and leaned against the wall. "That's for someone of a higher level to decide. I'm just supposed to make sure you're comfortable. And fed." She waved a hand at him again. "Go on, eat. The food here is amazing, wonderful."

"Give it a rest." Teo picked up the bowl of steaming sludge and scooped heaps of it into his mouth. He opened wide with the gunk oozing through his teeth and said, "Happy?" Some of it spilled onto his chest.

"So negative." Flora left the room and returned a moment later with a small towel. "You eat like a child, I'll treat you like a child." She patted the stains on his coverall. She must have used her extra credits to purchase perfume.

She smelled like she'd bathed in coconut oil. As she cleaned powdered food from Teo's collar, her breath mingled with his senses. Blood flooded the middle of his body. Flora stopped and glared at him. "You should be embarrassed."

Had she seen it? His eyes darted downward and back up long enough to confirm his coverall too bulky to allow his resurrection to announce itself. He adjusted his legs, to be safe.

When Flora finished, she took his empty bowl and stepped into the hallway. "Eat like a child again, I'll put in a request for you to be fed through a tube."

He didn't know what that meant. Contrary to his experience with arousal since the war, the physical manifestation of his excitement did not go away. He wanted to ask the orderly to take care of the task he believed she'd instigated. Then he asked himself:

Why the hell are you talking this way?

I'm horny.

My dick is hard.

I need some pussy.

Now.

"Get some sleep," said Flora. "Tomorrow's a big day." She flipped a switch in the hallway and the lights in Teo's room dimmed.

Teo lay back on his cot and put his hand between his legs. Taking care of himself would fill the room with evidence. Once puberty had hit, he'd never gone more than a week without either relieving himself or, as he got older, finding a woman to seduce. Memories of their faces, their bodies, their voices, the way they moved in the dark, all blended, all encouraged him to reach inside his coverall and reward his rediscovered libido. Whether or not he unzipped the front of his uniform, he did not know. His next conscious activity took place in the jungle, and then, in the crib, staring at the stuffed cheetah while two people screamed at each other, each promising the other murder.

A new orderly opened the door to Teo's room the following morning. Teo's skull felt as though it had been lodged in a vice grip. Fog filled his mind, as though he had not slept at all. The new orderly put a bowl of breakfast powder in front of him. Teo ate without being prompted. His mind and body had been drained, like he'd hiked the mountains in Big Bear. The new orderly stood by the door, said nothing. When Teo finished, he held the bowl out for the orderly to take.

"You can carry it yourself, my friend." The orderly told him to stand. "We're going for our first consultation with Dr. Cambio." He waited for him to do as instructed.

Teo's body ached as he unfolded himself from his seated position and joined the orderly. He glanced at the level five badge on the orderly's white coverall and the name underneath, Monte Ochoa. Then he took in the orderly's face and stopped himself from tripping over the foot of his bed. "Miguel?" He tried to force eye contact. "It's me, Teo."

The orderly stared out of the room, down the hallway. "We don't want to be late for Dr. Cambio." He nodded and urged Teo to follow him. "You can leave your bowl and spoon on any of the carts parked along the walls." He pointed to a metal ambulance stretcher. Several dirty bowls and spoons littered it.

"Miguel..." Teo spoke in a loud whisper. "Miguel, something's gone wrong. Very, very wrong."

"My name is Monte." He pointed to his ID badge. "Perhaps you don't know how to read, so I'll refrain from reporting you for attempting to misidentify me." He snapped his fingers at him without looking at him. "Let's go."

Teo dropped his bowl and spoon on the stretcher. He hurried behind Miguel, trying to think of a way to trap him into admitting his true identity. Their feet tapped the linoleum floors in rhythm, reminding Teo, once more, of the Blue Line to Long Beach, how the subway sounded like a train in an old Hollywood western. He remembered watching John Wayne movies with his father. His father told him the films had gotten history wrong. "But," he said, "when The Duke says, 'Print the legend,' he's talking about something greater than a choice on a government census form. He is talking about myth, about the stories keeping a culture stapled together over time. We may not like everything we see in these movies, but they belong to us. *All* of us. If we forget that, we shall have a world unlike anything we know or want."

The orderly escorted him to Franklin Hall. Teo knew this building well. At least, he had before the war. Most of his classes had been on the first floor. The sun tore through the classrooms during the day, making him uncomfortable while his professors implored him to feel angry for not having things rich people had. He'd bought into it. As a nineteen-year-old second-generation immigrant, he'd gotten furious any time he travelled too far west and encountered the slobs in Beverly Hills, their plastic skin drooping toward the floors of their BMWs and Porsches and Mercedes. The women waddled over sidewalks, their little handbags hoisted by their elbows. Oh, he bought right into it. Materialism, bad. Being broke and angry, good. Very, very good. When Dr. Rey and Dr. Lorca recruited students for a revolution, he didn't hesitate to sign up.

He wondered, as the orderly opened the door to a smaller classroom that had been converted to an office, how he'd been duped into yearning for a Cheetah 3000. The doctor, a woman in a black skirt and button-down white dress-shirt, stood with her back to him as she adjusted blinds on the windows. Without looking at him, she said, "Have a seat." She nodded her head at a vinyl couch across from a desk. Teo did as she asked and Miguel, now calling himself Monte, left the room and closed the door.

The woman took her time slanting the slats on the blinds so the sun's broken light on the floor stopped just before the couch and the desk. She strolled to her desk and sat in a high-backed leather chair. It squeaked anytime she moved. Teo wanted to read her ID badge, but she wore none.

He said, "Dr. Lorca?"

The woman faced him, her eyes straining over a pair of thin, round glasses. She pointed to her badge. "Dr. Cambio."

Absurd. "It's me," he said. "Teo. Teo Paz."

She rested her elbows on her desk and read his ID badge, then scraped a sheet of paper off her desk and compared whatever had been written on it with the badge. "Amazing," she said. "We have an amazing amount of work to do." She picked up a yellow pad of lined paper and began scribbling. "I suppose the sooner we figure out when this delusion started, the sooner we can figure out how to squash it."

"It's no delusion." Teo scooted forward. He spoke in a whisper. "I shot the mayor of Santa Barbara, on your orders, remember?"

This produced a flurry of writing from the doctor. She jotted down a page and a half of notes before responding. "You contend you, or this Teo Paz, was with the National Guard?"

"No, of course not." He fidgeted for a moment, a programmed response to being accused of barbaric ancestry. "My parents are from Guadalajara. I was born and raised in Los Angeles."

"So then," said the doctor, "why were you fighting for the north?"

He turned his head sideways, leaned closer. "Dr. Lorca, *you* gave the order to assassinate Mayor Martinez. Don't you remember?"

Another page of notes. The doctor looked up from the pad and said, "Why is it important for me to be part of your delusion?"

"Stop saying it's a delusion!" He clasped his hand over his mouth, as though that would reverse time and prevent the outburst.

"Thiago," said the doctor, "if you persist in negative behavior, I'll be forced to have you sedated."

Teo put his arms up on the couch, relaxed. "Dr. Lorca, why are you, why is Miguel, why are you all pretending you don't know me?"

"Who is Miguel?"

"The nurse, or whatever he's pretending to be, the guy who brought me to your classroom."

"My office?"

"This used to be a classroom."

More writing on the legal pad. Each time the doctor's pen slashed across the page, Teo imagined pieces of his brain hacked away with a machete. The doctor said, "So, Monte is really someone named Miguel. I'm a, what, former professor, somehow capable of ordering you to murder someone? And you are someone named Teo Paz?"

"Yes." Teo clapped his hands. "Thank you for being honest."

"Why is everyone pretending to be someone else?"

"I'm not."

"Okay. But everyone else is. What's the purpose?"

Again, Teo dropped his voice to a whisper. "I recently recovered a memory."

The doctor's left eyebrow raised. "Please."

"Well," said Teo, "you know about it. It's the assassination. In Santa Barbara. Someone, somewhere, after the war, implanted something in my jawbone to make me forget."

Shaking her head, grimacing, as though she'd just tasted the finest food on the planet, the doctor said, "This is a *rich* fantasy, Thiago."

"My name's not Thiago."

"Until I see official evidence otherwise, I'll be referring to you as Thiago."

Teo turned his head toward the windows. Did they have bars on the outside? If he jumped straight through them, how far would he get?

"When was this implant supposedly removed?"

He ran his fingers where the scar had been. "Few days ago."

"You had surgery? On your jaw?"

"Correct."

"You must have an amazing, wonderful immune system."

"They fixed it," he said. "The night they, I guess, drugged me? Took me to a different apartment. Gave me a different identity. They did something, I don't know what, to erase the wound, the scar."

"Who's *they*, Thiago?" She folded her hand holding her pen into a loose fist and rested her chin on it. Her grin reminded Teo of a cat, toying with its prey.

"Um, I guess…you." He knew where she would take things.

"Me?"

"You know what I mean."

"No, I don't." She returned to writing on her legal pad. "In order for us to help you establish your true identity, you're going to need to be as specific as possible."

"I'm not the one confused about my identity."

This produced a laugh the doctor quickly stifled. She shook her head as she scribbled on her pad. She reminded Teo of cold, cynical administrators at Los Angeles public schools he'd attended as a child. They wallowed in verbal virtue, parroting empty proclamations of compassion. If it came down to a teacher's word against a student's, these angels of tolerance always sided with the teacher.

"If you were healthy," she said, "you wouldn't be here."

"With all due respect," said Teo, "I'm here because I know something you don't want me talking about amongst the workers." There. He let it out. What could they possibly do to hurt him any more than they already had? Kill him? He'd welcome it. The architects of the revolution had made things worse than they'd ever been before the war.

"I'm curious," said the doctor. "Why would anyone else be threatened by your identity crisis?"

Teo forced himself to take a breath before responding. "If the workers knew the civil war started because of a lie, they might question the veracity of the Mutual Organization."

The doctor matched his patience. She pointed to his ID badge. "You're not a veteran, Thiago. Why do you think it's necessary for you to believe you had anything to do with the war?"

"Let me ask you something…"

She cut him off. "We're not here to discuss me, Thiago. We're here to discuss you, to get you back inside your own head."

He didn't know what to say. This woman he'd once looked up to, listened to, took orders from, had become a monolith for the Mutual Organization. As a result, she could not be honest. Could not be trusted. Talking with her in any meaningful manner made no sense. "Why do you think I would, as you put it, create a fantasy life where I fought in the war?"

Her shoulders slumped a bit, no longer made her posture so severe. "It's clear you're unimpressed with your own identity. The war fantasy allows you to believe your life is more important. In your case, you've constructed a simultaneously heroic and tragic history for yourself in which you are not only a veteran, but a veteran who's harbored a deep, conspiratorial secret."

Conspiracy.

Teo remembered the word from before the war. Questioning the official narrative always conjured it— "Enrique Cruz believes the government is intentionally poisoning the tap water in Los Angeles. He is a dangerous conspiracy theorist." And the public, programmed for years by mass media owned and controlled by international corporations, went along with the charade. It got to a point where they could label anyone a conspiracy theorist and the public, like Pavlov's dogs, salivated and volunteered their services as censors and witch hunters.

The doctor continued. "Thus, having braved the war and surviving is not heroic enough for you. Now, years after the end of the conflict, you must feed your ego with the ludicrous suggestion that you, in fact, instigated the war at the behest of your commanders. Your actions were not heroic, however, they were clandestine, so that now you may stake a claim to a different kind of heroism; you are the pawn, carrying a terrible secret, and by exposing this secret, you will be lauded in history as the man who brought down the, oh, let's give it an old world name, The System. You see? This is classic narcissism. And it's quite severe. Your name is right there on your chest, and you refuse to believe you are the person you've been identified as."

"That's all fascinating." Teo remembered similar conversations in college. He'd sit in a room full of people, most of them high on marijuana, throwing around wild speculation and allowing the imagination to accept it as intellectual investigation. His professors trained him to construe *anything* as oppressive—from government mandates to the price of tomatoes at different restaurants in different neighborhoods. Being forced to stand in line at a fast-food restaurant, under their tutelage, constituted some great, transgressive act on the part of the powers that be; these were *real* conspiracy theories. And they'd made him and his peers truly paranoid. "You still haven't told me why I would, to humor your allegiance to this process, create this fantasy."

"That's something we're going to have to discover together." She rested her pen on her desk, to the side of the legal pad. "We'll figure it out, Thiago. Something happened to you, at some point, something so terrible, you've risked offending the Mutual Organization to avoid confronting the pain caused by this event."

Teo returned to his room, escorted by Miguel. He tried once more to convince him to abandon the role he'd been assigned to play, to acknowledge their genuine identities. Miguel said, "Your troubles are amazing, my friend. But you will be cured. It will be wonderful, trust me."

The orderly locked the door from the outside, leaving Teo to sit by himself and stare at stark, white walls. The holding cells had once been offices for the professors at LACC. Posters of Che and Mao had adorned the walls, along with bookshelves filled with postmodern texts deconstructing everything from TV sitcoms to Barbie dolls. Nothing the old world had done, according to the great destroyers of Western Civilization, had been anything but oppressive. To a degree,

Teo still agreed. Why then, he wondered, had the Mutual Organization allowed for television to cross over into the New World? Technology had been deemed bad by the architects of the revolution. Dr. Rey had suggested technology distracted workers and made them slothful, useless. This allowed the oppressors to constantly shift their slave labor, replacing the affluent and lazy with hungry, impoverished men and women from so-called Third World countries. The professor had said, "The moment our ancestors picked up a rock and smashed open a walnut, something they could have done with their own hands and teeth, had they the patience, humanity began a parallel journey with technology that will lead us to a post-biological nightmare where we become the very circuits that make up the machines who will, in turn, replace the oppressors. If you think the patriarchy is bad, just wait until you're forced to confront a soulless machine. Complaints will never be heard. Those who risk engaging in complaint, by golly, the machines will grind them into dust."

It made sense. And yet, in post-Civil War South California, the Mutual Organization, upon deeper inspection, proved no less soulless than a machine. And unlike a machine, the Mutual Organization had been sloppy. They'd promised clean streets in downtown Los Angeles. Since the war, rats and coyotes, invited by neglect, felt no need to hide during daylight. They scoured the concrete for scraps with an arrogance suggesting they'd expected humans to let things go to such an extreme—layers of trash and rubble, set loose during combat and never attended to by the victors. And the workers went right on executing their robotic tasks. How many did what they were told while observing the mess, the hypocrisy, and said nothing? How much had to do with fear? What had kept Teo quiet? The implant in his jaw? Another example of technology the Mutual Organization found fit to use for their ends while concealing their hypocrisy.

He stared at the tiny window in his cell, the bars covering it. They probably wanted him to succumb to their programming or convince himself to go along with the illusion, to go back to working and pretending South California had achieved utopia.

Sunlight cutting through the bars on the window, painting stripes on the floor, only made him think of the word that had driven the revolution:

Freedom.

Dr. Rey, Dr. Lorca, and the rest of his professors had insisted he enjoyed no such privilege in the old world. The color of his skin imprisoned him from birth. Nothing he could do about it but overthrow the oppressors. He recalled conversations in classrooms where his professors talked and talked about the Great Enemy, but were never, when directly questioned, able to identify, in any empirical manner, who the oppressors were; once the war had been fought and the south had, conceivably, won, the reward had been identified as freedom. Teo rose from his bed and wrapped his fingers around two bars on his window. He tugged on them, tried to rip them from the wall. They wouldn't budge. Could the Mutual Organization be incompetent? Could they simply be unaware of what freedom actually looked like?

The door opened and Flora, now dressed in a coverall skirt revealing her sculpted, tanned legs, stepped into the room with a bowl of food. "It's that time of day." She nodded at his hands, still holding the bars on the window. "Are you being naughty?" She smirked and blushed. Had she become a different person? No longer the stern, mother-like authority figure demanding he eat his vegetables. "Have a seat." She pointed with her free hand at the bed.

One thought bulldozed everything else in Teo's mind:

I want to feast on this woman's thighs.
He imagined himself a wild animal, like a cheetah, eyeing its prey. Seeing a beautiful woman's skin accelerated his heartbeat, threatened to make him sweat. Blood rushed to his groin. He hurried to the bed to sit down before his desire became obvious. He crossed his legs, hoped that would settle his hormones. Instead, his coverall tightened as it stretched. The orderly offered him powdered food. Teo ate it in rapid gulps, hoping to finish and send her on her way before he said something and embarrassed himself.

The orderly said, "Slow down. You'll choke to death!" She did not speak in a manner suggesting concern, rather, more giggles and touching her chin with her index finger. If Teo didn't know better, he'd have confused her behavior for flirting.

"I apologize," he said. "The food is, you know, so wonderful…"

"Maybe you're getting better." The orderly sat next to him. The air filled with the scent of coconut oil. Teo thought of his grandpa, Enrique, telling stories of Tijuana and Club Hong Kong, where women smeared paint on their faces and drown in artificial fragrances and debased themselves for filthy American dollar bills. He spoke of a lesbian show in which two women lathered themselves with shaving cream and licked the cream off each other's bodies. He said he'd known several women who participated and developed throat cancer. These stories fueled Teo's belief in the sermons given by his women's studies professors at LACC. The Mutual Organization had done nothing, however, to discourage women from poisoning themselves to accommodate the fantasies of men.

Teo leaned away from her. He shoveled the food into his mouth and stared at the shadows on the floor. The orderly said, "What's the matter?" Her breath carried a cool, mint-laced aroma, begging Teo to snake his hand through her thick, black hair, and pull her in for a kiss. The woman laughed. Her dangling foot bounced to the rhythm of an unheard song. He finished the food and held the bowl toward her, still refusing to face her.

She took it from him. "Why won't you look at me?" Never had a question sounded so much like music. With her free hand, she straightened the skirt on her uniform. "Haven't worn one of these in a while," she said as she left the room.

The flat-tire staccato of Teo's heartbeat remained. Made him worry he might have a cardiac episode. Then a weight dropped on him and pushed him sideways, toward the plate-sized, uncomfortable pillow at the head of the bed.

He started in the jungle, again. This time, however, closer to the brush. Close enough he sensed the moisture on the leaves. Monkeys whooped in the distance. Frogs croaked. Underneath the wind massaging the towering Red Cedars, the growl of the cheetah reverberated, as though it were a part of the very land he could see, but not feel, under his feet. As the beast drew near, the air around him turned to lead, threatened to suffocate him. Despite having no sense of his physical being, he dreaded the pain the animal's teeth would generate the moment they landed in his imaginary flesh. He tried to close his eyes, or whatever allowed him to see his otherwise lush surroundings. Darkness did not follow, however. A flash, like one pass of a strobe light, and he found himself in the wooden cage.

His perception had altered since his last visit to this world, this place, lodged somewhere between waking and sleep. His vision morphed into something of a fish-eye view of the baby crib. Mammoth shadows of a man and a woman screaming at each other cut wild patterns in the light emanating from a ceiling he could not crane his head to see. And then he understood:

He had been placed *inside* the stuffed animal, the harmless toy cheetah.

When Miguel retrieved Teo the next morning for his session with Dr. Lorca, the orderly ducked in and removed what looked like a wire attached to the side of Teo's face with a circular, white sticky-pad. As though Teo had been hooked up to a machine while he slept. Miguel stuffed the item into the side pocket on his coverall. "Must be the janitor," he said. "Playing jokes on you while you rest, my friend."

Teo agreed. He walked with Miguel through the halls, toward Dr. Lorca's office. As they approached the office, however, he asked himself why he agreed. He had not been so amenable to any figure of authority since his liberation from the implant in his jaw. Taking a seat in the professor's office, he said to Dr. Lorca, "What are they doing to me while I sleep?"

The professor said she had no idea what he meant.

"Miguel, he removed something from my face just now. Something electronic."

"Oh, dear," said the professor. She took to writing on her notepad. "So, now, we're somehow molesting you while you sleep?"

"Your words," said Teo. "Not mine."

"You suggested…"

"No," said Teo. "You read into what I said. In fact, I would say, your response has revealed more than you should have." He held her glare, confident he'd shaken her.

The professor dashed a few sentences on her notepad. "Are you eating?"

"Excuse me?"

"Are you eating the food we're providing?"

"I don't have a choice."

"Very good." A second of mad slashings of her pen, and the professor said, "And what do you think of Flora, the orderly we've assigned to you at bedtime?"

"She usually comes in the afternoon." He realized he must have slept at least sixteen hours.

"Do you like her?"

"What do you mean?"

"Given the opportunity, would you perform procreational activities with her?"

"I'm not sure that's any of your business."

"I'm a doctor, Thiago," said the professor. "I'm here to heal you. Your mental and physical well-being are intertwined. I want to know that your procreational facilities are functioning."

"Then you should already know I was sterilized after the war."

The professor took a moment to process Teo's comment. "Ah, yes. The conspiracy fantasy." She flipped the pages on her notepad. "Yes, yes," she said. "You assassinated the mayor of Santa Barbara to inspire the south to take arms against the north." She looked up at him. "Stop me anytime I get the details of your delusion wrong."

"Calling the truth a delusion is wrong."

"Very well." She shuffled the pages of her notepad back to the top sheet. "So, explain to me, how you were, as you call it, sterilized."

"You gave the order," said Teo.

"Of course." The professor grinned. "I seemed to have an awful lot of power over you, Thiago."

"My name is Teo."

"Sure it is."

"You said, after the war, that I was too aggressive. That my genes needed to be, and these were your words, Dr. Lorca, you said my genes needed to be 'stopped in their tracks.' You then sent me to another office where they injected something into my arm and I could no longer maintain a, you know, an erection." He felt stupid, talking about sex in such hygienic terms. A woody. A chubby. A boner. He couldn't keep it up, goddammit. Barely thirty years old (as far as he knew), and he couldn't keep his motor running long enough to satisfy a woman.

"So," the professor said, "you can't become aroused, yes? The Mutual Organization has deprived you of the obligation of procreational activities?"

"You won't let me fuck," said Teo.

The professor blushed. Hardly an appropriate reaction for someone whose profession once specialized in the removal of stigma from all sexual pursuits. She said, "Have you tried?"

He told her about his night with his former supervisor. The professor attempted to tell him no such person could exist since Thiago Puga could not possibly have worked in a supermarket. He cut her off and finished his story.

"Your penis becomes aroused," the professor said, "but doesn't stay so enough to penetrate a woman?"

Teo nodded.

"Is it possible you don't prefer…"

"Not a chance."

"You never quite answered my original question." The professor made a few notes. "Have you actually tried to penetrate a woman since, according to your delusion, the end of the war?"

"I did answer," said Teo. "And the answer is, before I could slide inside her, I remembered you sterilized me, and my penis went to sleep."

"Then it's a mental issue."

Teo had never considered the possibility. He stifled the urge to argue.

"Do you masturbate?" said the professor.

"What would be the point?"

"Indeed," said the professor. "The Mutual Organization doesn't encourage anything that might impair the creation of a future worker." She wrote some more and changed the subject. "How are you sleeping these days?"

"Okay, I suppose."

"Do you dream?"

"I think so."

"What are some recent dreams you can recall?"

"I've been having the same dream about being in a jungle and then, for some reason, in a baby crib."

"Fascinating," said the professor. "What else is going on around you in the dreams?"

"I'm running from a cat, a big cat. A cheetah."

This inspired a flurry of notes from the professor.

Teo said, "And then, in the crib, there's a stuffed cheetah. A toy. I can hear people in the background, sometimes see them."

"Who are they?"

"A man and a woman." His throat dried. He wanted to cry. He pulled up his nose and straightened his shoulders, as though his ego had been challenged. "They're fighting. Cussing. Screaming at each other. It sounds like they want to kill each other."

The professor shook her head as she jotted information on her notepad. "Who are these people, these people fighting?"

"I don't know."

She stopped dabbing at her notepad like a butcher slicing beef and looked at him. "Really?"

He said nothing.

"Thiago, you realize, we figure out who these people are, we will understand why you've invented an alternate reality you seem unable to escape."

"My name's Teo," he said.

She composed more pages of notes.

Teo waited for his food. Several rats outside his window hissed, suggesting a turf war might be taking place. The door to his room opened and Flora, now dressed in a pink coverall, the hem barely passing her pelvic region, stepped in with a steaming bowl in her hands. She set the bowl on a shelf by the door and sat next to Teo on his bed. "Dr. Cambio tells me you believe you cannot make love to a woman." For a moment, she flashed him a flat face, no emotion. He supposed this must be the look a woman at Club Hong Kong donned before climbing the stage and covering herself with shaving cream. "You look healthy to me." She squeezed his upper arm. "Big, strong guy like you," she said. "I'll bet you can send a girl right over the moon." In another time and place, an enthusiastic woman might have delivered this dialogue in a singsong, seductive tone. Flora's tone reminded Teo of the robotic voices of telephone operators from before the war.

He started to speak, started to tell Flora she didn't have to do anything she didn't want to. She pushed his mouth closed with her fingers and kissed his neck. He had no trouble getting aroused (*a chubby*, goddammit, *a hard on!*) and stared at himself in awe as the woman undressed him and his mind and body stayed on task. Before long, he took over, tearing the buttons off her coverall, and made love to her...fucked her, goddammit, he *FUCKED* her.

Teo felt wonderful the following morning. Amazing and wonderful. He remembered making love to...*fucking*, *banging*, *humping*...the beautiful orderly, Flora. Thinking of her coconut-flavored skin against his aroused him again. He wanted to masturbate, an activity he hadn't engaged in to completion since before the war. He wanted to close his eyes and remember her on top of him, staring down at him with a smile unhindered by ulterior motives. She appeared unburdened, thrilled with life, alleviating the pain of mortality with the one activity adults could call play. Being with her reminded him of the last woman he'd successfully completed the act with—A classmate named Nadia, in college. He'd met her during a meeting conducted by Dr. Rey and Dr. Lorca. Like so many women, she decorated her body with a tattoo. A cheetah, on her lower back. He'd asked her about it but had no recollection of her responding. He also couldn't recall much beyond the sex with Flora. She'd insisted he eat his cold, soggy food afterward. Then he'd been in the crib, in the eye of the stuffed cheetah, scared out of his mind as the screaming giants battled closer and closer to the wooden bars surrounding him.

And he understood: Flora, per order of the Mutual Organization, no doubt, had drugged him. She must have done so every night. They were tampering with him. Again. As always. Must have had something to do with the node attached to his temple the previous morning. This somewhat quelled the passion brought on by the memory of holding Flora, tasting her breath, feeling her thighs quiver against his. This tempered the illusion, the belief she'd enjoyed the experience as much as he had. When Monte (Miguel, *dammit*, the man's name is Miguel) retrieved him for his session with Dr. Lorca, he attempted, once more, to compel Miguel to admit his role in the ruse. He first goaded him, saying, "You look amazingly haggard." He pointed to Miguel's eyes, the dark rings bordering them. "You look as though you haven't slept wonderfully in days. As though, perhaps, thoughts plague your mind."

Miguel said, "My friend, can we make this journey through the corridor without your wonderfully amazing, psychotic delusions?"

Teo followed him into the hallway. He walked a few feet behind him, in case his chiding prompted the orderly to turn around and punch him. Such a gesture, in fact, would be a victory. It would prove he'd gotten underneath Miguel's skin, forced the remorse he must have felt by his betrayal. He said, "Do they reprogram you? Entirely, I mean?" He ran his fingers over his head, pantomimed a surgeon, or a mechanic, working on a brain, or a car engine. Miguel didn't turn around to witness the performance. Teo continued, "That's what they're trying to do to me, isn't it? When they knock me out with, well, with whatever drugs they use to…"

Wagging a lone finger in Teo's face, Miguel said, "My friend, I will ask you one more time to cease including me in your fantasies. Should you refuse to heed my request, I will employ amazingly violent means to shut your mouth."

"Feeling guilty?" Teo may or may not have finished his sentence. Miguel's fist landed across the bridge of his nose. He went into a lucid shock, aware his mind had produced chemicals to distract him from the pain. Blood spurted from his nostrils. He held his hand over his nose and spoke in nasal tones. "This will be interesting," he said, thinking about the explanation the orderly would offer Dr. Lorca. "If I'm not mistaken, your job is to protect patients, yes?"

The orderly ducked into a utility closet and emerged with a white towel. He tossed it at Teo. "Apologies, my friend," he said. "Your ability to annoy is wonderful. Amazing. Now, clean yourself up for the doctor."

Once seated on Dr. Lorca's couch, jamming the towel against his face, Teo said, "You're not going to win. You know that, right?"

She chastised Miguel for losing his temper and dismissed him for the day. "Come back," she said to him, "when you're capable of conducting yourself in the humane manner the Mutual Organization expects from its workers." She assured him he would be docked credits, credits she knew he'd hoped for in his attempts to save for a Leopard 200, whatever that might have been. She picked up her pad and began writing. "I see you're still clinging to your illusion…"

"What are you doing to me at night?" Teo spoke in a muffled voice through the towel.

"Excuse me?" Dr. Lorca scribbled on her pad.

"Last night, after you had Flora seduce me…"

The doctor sat straight. She placed her pen and pad on her desk and adjusted her glasses. "I'm sorry, what did you just say?"

Teo lifted the towel from his mouth. Crusted blood flaked off his lips as he spoke. "You sent Flora into my room, my prison cell, to have sex with me."

She wrote like a poet in an inspirational fever. "Wait a minute, Thiago…I thought…" She flipped back several pages and read her notes. "I thought we sterilized you, correct? You're unable to maintain a state of arousal long enough to penetrate a woman. This is your story, don't forget." She returned to the page on which she'd been writing. "When Flora, as you say, seduced you, did you not fail to maintain your erection?"

Such sterile language. No wonder the previous world collapsed. What kind of people derived so little pleasure from life they assigned stuffy verbiage to the most interesting activity adults engaged in? They'd turned natural communication into an academic exercise, something to be studied, like the nervous system on a frog. To make damn sure he had her attention, he said, "I fucked her brains out."

First the woman dropped her jaw, then her pen. An obvious performance. She snapped her neck, moved her head left and right, as though shaking the outrage from her ears like unwanted dust. "Thiago, I'm willing to work with you, help you through this, but you must show me some level of respect."

"I'm being honest with you, Dr. Lorca. That's the highest level of respect a human being can show another."

"Such profanity, though…" She stopped, looked confused. "Dr…Oh, yes, I'm, ah, this Dr. Lorca character in your drama. Yes, yes. Well, what I wanted to say was, the outlawed word you employed, it denotes an inability to express yourself in a more meaningful manner."

"Bullshit." The use of the ancient, forbidden terms felt more liberating than fucking the deceitful Flora. "These words were outlawed because they allowed individuals to express themselves in the rawest manner. They allowed human beings to be human beings. You, and even the power structure before you, want human beings to be obedient workers and consumers. For that to happen, you must control the way they think and the last door between you and the mind of an individual is speech. You regulate speech, you regulate thought, because now the individual must spend his thoughts on how to express himself without offending those who determine what is and isn't so-called acceptable speech. At that moment, you've intruded upon the individual's mind, upon his thoughts, and altered him."

Dr. Lorca grinned. "You remind me of a junior high student, desperate to escape the conformity becoming an adult requires."

"Don't give me that shit." Teo put down the towel and stared at the woman until she blinked.

"Very well." She resumed writing. "We're not here to discuss individuality, Thiago. We're here to discuss your psychological condition. And, frankly, I want to hear about this latest installment in your fantasy—that our orderly, Flora, seduced you and, am I correct, you completed the act?"

Teo crossed his arms. "You didn't hear her wild, spastic screams of delight?"

"Well, I'm confused, Thiago…"

"Teo."

"Thiago." She adjusted her glasses. "According to the story you've been pitching here, you're unable to have sex."

"You certainly made me believe I'd been sterilized."

"If," said the woman, "you completed the act with Flora, we must conclude you have *not* been sterilized. I mean, let's talk pure, empirical science here… You penetrated her. You did precisely what you claimed you could not. What…*Teo Paz* could not do."

Teo remained quiet.

"Is it possible," said Dr. Lorca, "that Thiago Puga was *not* sterilized, hence, Thiago Puga's ability to sustain an erection and make love to Flora Curadora?"

Teo protested.

"Stay with me, Thiago," said Dr. Lorca. "If one of the most fundamental dimensions of the identity you've invented and seem determined to uphold is non-existent, doesn't it follow that the *entire* mirage you've created is just that? Meaning, *non-existent*? Meaning, your virility proves you are *not* Teo Paz."

"Forget it, Dr. Lorca." Teo leaned back. "These games might work with others. Obviously, they worked with Miguel. My mind is free."

"How do you explain your ability to make love to a woman, now?"

He knew the Mutual Organization had something to do with it. Perhaps vitamins they'd put in the slop they fed him, along with the sleeping agent. He kept it to himself, however, knowing the doctor would deny it. He said, "I don't know." An ill wave passed through his blood. A man of honor engaging in an act of deliberate dishonesty, it seemed, caused physical discomfort.

A different orderly led Teo back to his room. Taller, wider. Identified by his badge as Jorge Suplento. On the walk through the hallway, he put his arm around Teo's shoulder and said, "Let us establish a wonderful, amazing agreement." He grinned, raised his eyebrows a few times. His silver and gold teeth reflected lights from the ceiling. "You keep your anti-social mumbling to yourself, and I don't finish what Monte started this morning."

"What did Miguel start?" said Teo.

The orderly chuckled. He shook his head, resembled a disgruntled parent attempting to channel instructions to a stubborn child. "You see? You've provided a wonderful example of what I'm talking about."

"I don't get it." Teo shrugged hard enough to throw the orderly off his shoulder.

The orderly resituated his grip, this time vice-gripping his fingers around Teo's upper arm. "Your amazing capacity for disingenuous conversation might fascinate the doctor, the other staff members here. It does the opposite of amuse me. It infuriates me." He stopped and leaned close, so that only Teo would hear him. "Had I been in Monte's shoes this morning, why, my friend, I would have pushed your dense skull straight through the wall." He smiled once more and urged Teo to continue walking toward his room.

Teo said, "If I'm not mistaken, you're exhibiting highly negative behavior. I was under the impression the Mutual Organization didn't encourage such..."

Jorge clutched a fistful of Teo's hair and yanked his head backward. "In the service of the Mutual Organization, I will do whatever it takes to neutralize troublemakers like you."

They spent the rest of the journey to Teo's room in silence. The old rage, the inability to control himself when confronted by bullies, bubbled in his heart. If the orderly believed he could overpower him without a fight, he would have himself a wonderful, amazing surprise. He wished the man well as he stepped into his room.

"There's a good attitude." Jorge closed the door and locked it from the outside. Teo stood in the middle of the room, his attention turning to the caged window. He tried once more to jostle the bolts holding the bars in place. Impossible. He tired and sat on the bed. As he lay sideways and allowed himself to sleep, the door opened and another orderly entered. Not Flora. An older woman. She carried a tray with a steaming bowl of slop on it.

"Time for dinner." She held the tray in one hand and gave Teo's thigh a gentle tap. Green cables of veins on the backs of her hands suggested she'd traveled well past middle age. She'd dyed her hair red and painted her eyelids the same color. Her voice croaked across a throat Teo suspected coated with tar and nicotine from a pre-war cigarette habit. He wanted to ask her, to confirm his suspicion. And, had she been a smoker, did she miss the cigarettes? What would she be willing to do to regain the freedom to choose to destroy her lungs? Studying the concrete stillness in her eyes, a sign of dedication to her work, he opted, instead to say:

"A little early for dinner." He sat up and pointed to the window, moved his finger along the beam of sunlight painting an orange rectangle on the floor.

The woman rasped a couple of laughs and placed the tray and the bowl on top of it in front of him. "Eat up, honey." Her badge identified her as Seha Choi. Her perfume smelled like a patch of gardenias. The tray hovered under Teo's nose until he took the bowl and spoon next to it in his hands. "Very good," said the woman.

Teo shoveled the slop into his mouth. He needed the woman to leave while the food sat in his belly in a heap. He polished off the bowl and thanked her. "Will you be the new orderly at night?" he said. The woman confirmed. "Any idea what happened to Flora?"

"Who is that?" said the woman.

Teo lay back down. "I'm feeling tired." He waved his hand toward the door, suggesting the woman be on her way.

"Very good," she said.

Once the woman's padded footsteps faded down the hall, Teo stood. He pulled the bed away from the wall and knelt near the corner. He tickled the back of his throat with his index finger. He hadn't done anything so silly since grade school, when he wanted to convince his father he'd caught a bug and couldn't attend classes. He did his best to stifle his gagging until the garbage he'd eaten rushed back up. He heaved against the wall and jumped as his vomit splattered into a puddle in the corner. Satisfied he'd ridden himself of the bogus food, he resituated the bed and pretended to sleep.

Having reached a point where he found no surprise by the actions of the Mutual Organization, he remained still when, an hour later, the door to his room opened. He kept his eyes closed. He heard something rolled next to the bed, the shuffling of feet around him. Hands nudged him, perhaps making sure the drugs had taken effect. As someone attached nodes to his temples, to his chest, arms, and legs, he resisted the urge to laugh as fingers accidentally tickled him. Unseen villains positioned his head to face the ceiling while others placed a heavy apparatus over his upper body. A syringe entered his arm and he could not stop himself from opening his eyes.

He sat in the giant crib, inside the stuffed cheetah. The silhouettes of a man and a woman gesticulated against a bare wall beyond the wooden bars of the crib. Their shouting morphed into growls appropriate for a monster. He raised his hands, felt the apparatus covering his face, and ripped it off. The light from his room temporarily blinded him. As his vision adjusted, three doctors in coats scrambled to remove the nodes attached to him and escape undetected. He leapt from his bed and slammed the door shut, trapping them. He spoke in a deep, aggressive voice he hadn't used in, he imagined, a decade:

"What the *fuck* is going on?"

Six orderlies subdued him. He kicked, threw punches. They took them with grunts, occasionally wiping their own blood from their eyes. They did not strike back. They overpowered him, each grabbing an arm or leg, the fifth placing wrench-like fingers around his neck. The sixth orderly directed them through the hallway. They carried him down a flight of steps, his limbs flailing as he tried to free himself, through a corridor whose floor, ceiling, and walls, appeared to be made of stainless steel, and into a room with a lone chair bolted to the floor. They secured his limbs with leather straps. They employed a fifth belt to force his head to stay in one position, his eyes to see in a single direction. He unloaded every forbidden word he could think of, as though the rage they stood in place of would provide fuel needed to combat the orderlies, all of whom looked to outweigh him by at least fifty pounds. Once they'd imprisoned him in the bolted chair, he caught his breath. His chest heaved as the men backed away and, he guessed, exited the room. In front of him, the only place his eyes could gather information, a window the length of the wall held his attention as a light in the room on the other side of the window turned on and invited him to consider someone in an orange jumpsuit, the kind appropriate for a prisoner in the old California penal system. The shape of the person suggested a woman. She'd been fitted with a black, cloth sack over her head. Ropes kept the sack in place and, upon squinting, Teo saw rope had also been used to tie the woman's hands behind her. The woman paced from one side of the long, bare room to the other. She reminded Teo of sitcoms in the old world, of expectant fathers in a hospital, waiting on news of freshly born offspring. He wondered who, between the two of them, might be in the worse position.

How much time passed? No clocks in the room. At least, none he could see. No windows to the outside world, no idea whether night had fallen. Maybe he'd been there longer? The woman in the other room hypnotized him, marching back and forth, back and forth, like a stopwatch on a chain. She eventually tired and sank from view. Did she sleep right there, on the hard, tiled floor? Fatigue washed over him and he slipped into hypnagogia. Lucid dreams of his past played before him—the nonchalant manner he'd approached life until college. Nothing carried much gravity. Then college. Nadia. The cheetah on her lower back, above her right cheek, glowing, in the dark, as she heaved with passion. A woman's voice spoke to him, said "It's unfortunate we've come to this."

Dr. Lorca. Teo opened his eyes, forced himself to wake up. The doctor's musky perfume greeted his senses. She stepped around the front of the chair. She cradled her notebook in one arm. She clicked her pen with her other hand. Nervous. Before she spoke again, he said:

"What kind of technology do you have here?"

She said nothing.

"The Mutual Organization promised us such things had been banned. Outlawed."

The doctor opened her notepad and scribbled on it. "Teo…"

He tried to sit up. The restraint across his forehead snapped him back into place. "I thought…"

She nodded. "Everything you suspect," she said, "is true. We manipulated you as a student. We attempted to do so after the war. It's imperative we reprogram you now and send you back into the general population. You are one of the last deadeyes in South California. Just as the first American civil war was the result of the Mexican American war, a war fought not twenty years before the conflict between the states, we are certain the north will try, once again, to impose their will on us. We cannot afford to lose a marksman such as yourself."

"I refuse." He couldn't shake his head to punctuate his conviction.

"Teo…" The doctor spoke quietly, as though she worried someone might hear. As though she had reason to fear. "With all that you've discovered, do you still believe you have *any* say in what happens to you?"

"Give me a fair fight," he said. "Let's see what happens." His father taught him to reserve violence for conflicts with other men. Women were to be dealt with verbally. But he could now see himself pushing Dr. Lorca to the ground if needed. She had not earned his respect, his ingrained reverence for the female of the species.

The doctor disappeared for a moment and returned. The light in the room beyond the window brightened. "Perhaps I spoke in haste, Teo." She directed his attention to the performance in the other room. Two men in black coveralls, the kind worn by the men who'd brought him to Identity Adjustment, entered. They picked up the woman who'd been pacing and, Teo assumed, worn herself out and decided to nap. One held her arms behind her back while the other ripped off her orange jumpsuit. Dr. Lorca said, "This is a demonstration, Teo. You must decide whether you prefer a similar fate." He did not respond. He could not respond. As the inspectors in the other room turned the naked woman to face him, the mystery of Ji Young's disappearance ceased. The tattoo of the bobcat on her inner thigh quivered, revealed her fear.

"Please," said Teo. "I'll be whoever you want me to…"

"Let's make sure," she said.

The inspectors glanced at the doctor. She nodded. The man who'd undressed Ji Young produced a pistol from a front pocket on his coverall. The gun had a long barrel. An odd, rectangular grip. He joined the other man behind Ji Young and placed the barrel of the gun against the back of her head. The glass separating the rooms did nothing to muffle the highest notes of her shriek. And then a pop, a familiar sound from the war. The men ducked as blood splashed toward them and splattered the glass. Ji Young dropped to the floor in the middle of her scream. Her final, honest judgment of the Mutual Organization.

The ride on the transport from Highland Park to the trash heap near Hollywood generally took thirty minutes. Thiago Puga, thus, awoke and attended to his morning routine two hours before the Mutual Organization required him to swipe his ID badge and get to work scavenging recyclable material. He boiled water on the stove while he sat on the toilet on the opposite side of the apartment. The morning news broadcast on the television commanded his attention, distracted him from a constant, low-key buzz in his right ear. He mixed some of the water with breakfast powder and used the rest to fill the basin next to his toilet. As the water in the basin cooled, he stirred and ate the breakfast powder. It tasted like nothing, which pleased him. Lack of variety, difference, could not have been more wonderful, more amazing. On the television, images of violent clashes between warring tribes in the north reminded him how lucky he had it, living in the south, where the Mutual Organization had solved the problem of human aggression and created the perfect society. Utopia, educated folks called it, before his time. The newscaster, the current version of Maya Minassian, said so. She said, after the montage of barbaric behavior concluded, "So grateful for the sacrifice of our soldiers in the Civil War. I can walk the streets at night and feel safe." Thiago agreed. The notion he should have fought in the war nagged. He shuffled the thought into the same dead zone he stored knowledge of the annoying buzz in his ear. To express it in negative terms, he *ignored* it.

After scrubbing himself with a moist washcloth, he put on a beige coverall. The closet sunk into the wall near the toilet contained seven coveralls, each the same color. Eventually, he would rise above his level and be allowed to choose which color he wore on a day-to-day basis. In the meantime, same uniform, different day. He slipped his feet into his heavy, industrial boots and tied the laces. Grime and guts and other waste had crusted onto their rubber tracts. He would have to scrub them in his basin, soon. As he clipped his ID badge to his uniform and prepared to leave his apartment, a commercial for a Bobcat 5000 played on the television. A sleek, box-like car, painted black and gold, cruising through canyons and across mountain ranges Thiago assumed, without resentment, he would never see. The car itself, he could obtain. Rising to a higher level and improved credit condition would secure him the Bobcat 5000 in due time. "Let patience be your ally," he told himself. He turned off the television, still marveling at the footage of the Bobcat 5000 streaking over American highways, the ultimate symbol of liberty. "Wonderful," he said, imagining himself behind the wheel, gloves on his hands, like an old-fashioned racecar driver. "Amazing."

On the transport to the trash heap, Thiago shared a bench with a fellow level one, a woman he'd seen collecting rat carcasses off the streets of downtown L.A. They bobbed their heads in rhythm with "Sunshine Manifesto," playing on the transport's radio. The driver had the courtesy to push the volume, rendering conversation impossible. Every time the song finished the DJ said, "That was your favorite and mine, 'Sunshine Manifesto.' And now for something wonderful and amazing, 'Sunshine Manifesto!'" And Thiago and his neighbor on the bus nodded their heads once more. The comfort of familiarity, the peace of mind accompanying the knowledge that nothing he couldn't control would ever change, made him feel secure. Thoughts of mortality and other dangers would never plague him. The mind could relax in such a nurtured environment. Only work and rest mattered. New ideas, they brought pain and misfortune to those foolish enough to entertain them.

The transport rumbled through downtown, through Koreatown, made its stops. Passengers shuffled on and off, and in an amount of time he felt, in his bones, too soon, arrived at the trash heap. He could not, of course, voice this concern. It would be construed as a complaint. He'd listened to workers engage in such negativity. They usually disappeared, which suggested they'd been reduced to level zeroes and forced to stand on an assembly line in a dank, suffocating factory on the other side of town. The transport turned north and then west on Santa Monica. The ruins of buildings destroyed during the civil war gave way like a massive, intricate entrance, and there stood the trash heap, a beast made of human and animal waste. Its apex already appeared taller than Thiago's apartment building. Yellow and black Mutual trucks from all around South California delivered loads of refuse. Stationary cranes scooped from their dump boxes and swung high until finding a suitable spot to drop the load and add to the blossoming mountain. The trash had been distributed in such a way as to allow the gradual creation of a spiral path leading up and down. Level ones made their way in groups, each fitted with a sectioned hemp bag draped around their necks. They used sanctioned poles with sharp ends to sift through the fresh garbage and pierce anything recyclable. For glass, they leaned over and picked it up with hands protected by sturdy gloves the Mutual Organization allowed them to rent.

Thiago stepped off the transport. The steaming morning sun added to his carousel of thoughts and emotions. Sweat formed at his temples and the back of his neck. Had the trash heap not smelled so wonderfully awful, he would have been equally repelled by the odor his own body produced. He allowed an inspector at the gate to examine his ID badge. The inspector nodded and said, "Wonderful morning, yes?"

"Amazing," said Thiago. "Wonderful and amazing." He followed his coworkers, some he'd seen before, others who carried hints of disgust in the downward lines on their faces. Perhaps they'd been demoted to a lower level. This meant positions at higher levels might be available. Thiago walked faster, eager to rent his gloves, choose a sack and spear from the tool shed at the base of the mountain, and impress the inspectors with his enthusiasm.

The first three stories of the mountain had been picked clean. Occasional scraps of paper or plastic cups or bowls might spill from above. Workers hiking the path to the fresh clumps of recyclable waste competed to jab anything they could stuff in their bags and demonstrate to the inspectors how thrilled they were to work. Thiago walked on the outside, near the edge. He didn't bother with the vulture-like attack on lone plates or forks. He kept his eye on the downward slope to his right, looking for something particularly reckless discarded by someone from a higher level. He would bag it and show it to the inspectors upon returning at the end of the day. The Mutual Organization accepted people would toss out their plastic dining utensils and even the emptied boxes of food powder. Sometimes, however, someone from a much higher level would break the remote control for their television and attempt to hide it in their regular trash. A find such as this would earn Thiago praise from the inspectors and, he believed, help him advance one step closer to owning a Bobcat 5000.

Drenched in sweat, he finally reached the newer additions to the mountain. The sweat stung his eyes. He forced himself to conflate the pain with pleasure. His fellow level ones teetered across fresh, moist terrain. Here lurked the bodies of expired animals and expired citizens. Thiago felt the bones of human corpses, most of them quite old. His foot slipped every so often and he sank to his knees in garbage. He'd land the spear in a sturdier, fresher body and hoist himself back to the surface. He pushed and nudged the corpses to see if the dead concealed anything valuable beneath them. On this day, he stumbled over the decaying body of a woman whose shoulder-length black hair had not ceased growing despite a gash of flesh taken from her skull. Her death must have been horrible. Violent. Perhaps she'd been murdered by a barbarian from the north. The Mutual News suggested such things happened as the north, unhappy with the results of the war, wanted a rematch. The woman had been stripped nude. Her skin had turned gray. Thiago wedged his spear under the woman's rigid flesh and turned her over. Damage done by time and animals scouring the garbage heap at night had not obscured the tattoo of a bobcat on the woman's left, inner thigh. The tattoo reminded Thiago of a series of sessions he'd had with an identity specialist. He'd dreamt of a cheetah. The psychologist revealed the cheetah represented his parents, who'd nearly killed each other on the way to a divorce. He'd been a toddler when the split occurred. And, according to the doctor, split best described his toddler mind's response. He imagined himself hidden, inside a stuffed cheetah in his crib. Until the doctor explained what had happened, he'd lived a confused life. Since those sessions, he'd found amazing, wonderful ease with his identity as a level one.

He returned his attention to the dead woman. Her remaining eye had not closed. Its brown hue had not dulled as her skin had; she stared at the polluted sky with a question in her gaze that would never be answered. Her body had been placed over the frayed remains of a blue coverall. Thiago tilted the woman's corpse off the fabric and lifted the uniform with the end of his spear. Maybe hers? A plastic ID badge remained fastened to it. No. The uniform had belonged to a man. He brought the coverall closer and unclipped the ID badge. The plastic sheath holding it could be recycled. He removed the card inside revealing the owner's name, level, and visage. After dropping the plastic sheath into his hemp bag, he started to crumple the actual ID to stuff it into the section of his bag reserved for paper products. The picture on the ID, however, beckoned him to stop. He examined the badge. It belonged to someone named Teo Paz, level three. He stared at the picture. Ice raced through his blood, forced him to steady himself as his body shivered. He glanced at the ID badge on his uniform, and back at the picture on the ID he'd removed from the plastic sheath. The pictures were the same.

The exact same.

His sweat oozed faster, thicker. He wiped his forehead and considered the possibility he had an identical twin who'd passed on and Thiago happened to be the worker on the mountain responsible for recycling his badge. The scarier idea, of course, being Thiago and this Teo Paz shared the same body, the same mind. What avenues of negative thought might such an investigation lead to? What disruptions in his desire to advance to a level three, to a job not requiring constant cleaning of the tracts on his boots?

Thiago squeezed the paper ID in his hand, turned it into a tiny ball, and dropped it into the appropriate section of his hemp sack. He would dump the contents of his hemp sack in the piles at the bottom of the mountain, say nothing to the inspectors, go home, watch television, and forget he'd ever seen the suspicious badge. He would be Thiago Puga, as the Mutual Organization obviously desired, and cheerfully work his way through whatever life they deemed appropriate for him.

Ronin Heck is a professor of philosophy from the great state of Minnesota.

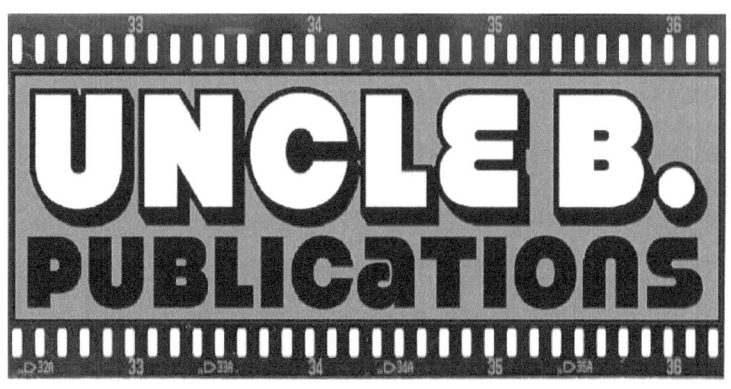

AN INDIANAPOLIS BASED PUBLISHING MAFIA
and
PROUD MEMBER
of the

Wherever GOOD BOOKS Are Sold!

www.ingramcontent.com/pod-product-compliance
Lightning Source LLC
Chambersburg PA
CBHW030351180626
46812CB00007B/2843